MW00479627

JAPANESE MYTHOLOGY

Classic Stories of Japanese Myths, Gods, Goddesses,

Heroes, and Monsters, The Story of Princess Hase,

Issun-Boshi, Momotaro, Kintaro, Kaguya Hime

ROBERTS PARIZI

TABLE OF CONTENTS

INTRODUCTION

First off, I would like to thank you for choosing this book. I hope that whether you choose it for purely entertainment purposes or a learning experience, that it does just that.

This book is filled with Japanese myths and folktales that will teach you a bit about their culture and keep you entertained for hours. Japanese mythology isn't one of your mainstream mythologies unless you are already into Japanese culture, anime, and the like. I'm glad you have found yourself here, though, as Japanese mythology is so unique and diverse.

If you are familiar with any of their myths, there is a good chance you may find that some of these stories are slightly different. That's because the various regions of Japan, back before it became so populated, created their own versions of the stories to match their uniqueness. Plus, you have the Shinto and Buddhist influence in the various myths and tales.

Before we get into the stories, though, we will cover the history of Japanese mythology, along with the Kamis, and essential words that will help with the comprehension of the stories.

One last thing before we begin, if you find any part of this book helpful or entertaining, I ask that you please leave a review.

CHAPTER 1

The History of Japanese Mythology

Japanese mythology is a bunch of stories that were created from oral traditions that had been passed down through the generations that talked about the history of their people, practices, customs, ceremonies, gods, and legends. Japanese mythology has a long history that dates back over 2000 years. It was transformed into two main religions. One is an indigenous religion called Shinto. The other was Buddhism that was created in India and was brought into Japan from Korea and China.

Their mythology includes many spirits, goddesses, and gods. Most of these stories talk about how the world was created, how the islands of Japan were formed, and all the activities of the magical creatures, spirits, animals, humans, and deities. Some were set in locations like the underworld and heaven.

Japanese Myth Sources

Most of these myths that have survived the times have been recorded in the *Nihonshoki* and the *Kojiki*. The *Kojiki* was created for the imperial court. It houses the world's creation, how the gods originated, and the Japanese emperors' ancestry. They claim to have descended from Amaterasu, the sun goddess. These books told of the ruling class's origins and were used to strengthen their authority. Because of this, these aren't pure myths but have been colored by politics. These have been based on two traditions: The Izumo Cycle and the Yamato Cycle. The Izumo Cycle is based on the character of Susanoo no Mikoto, who is Amaterasu's brother. They Yamato Cycle is based on Amaterasu Omikami, the sun goddess.

The *Nihonshoki* was finished in 720 and contained many legends and myths. It also helps to establish the Imperial family's genealogy. The *Nihonshoki* was influenced a lot by Korean and Chinese mythology and history. Both the *Nihonshoki* and the *Kojiki* contain some elements of Taoism. This is a Chinese religion that was brought to Japan in the 600s.

Mythological records and genealogies were kept from about the 700s and possibly a lot longer than that. By Emperor Temmu's time, which was in the 800s, it was necessary to know all the members in the families who were important so they could establish their positions for each one in the eight levels of title and rank that was created based on the Chinese court system. Because of this, Temmu ordered them to create books about the genealogies and myths that resulted in the *Nihonshoki* and *Kojiki*. The people who made these and other documents had all the documented and oral sources at their disposal. There were more sources available to the people who created the *Nihonshoki*. Even though the *Kojiki* has more myths and genealogy in it, the *Nihonshoki* gives more understandings of both their folklore and the history of early Japan. The primary purpose of it was to provide the Sinicized court a history that they could compare with the Chinese annals.

Major Characters and Deities

The reason behind creating the *Nihonshoki* and the *Kojiki* was to trace the imperial genealogy all the way back to the creation of the world. You can find the Yamato Cycle myths easily in these accounts. At the beginning of the world, it was a vast mass, a dark ooze that was filled with seeds. Slowly, the fine particles turned into heaven or yang, and the massive particles turned into earth or yin.

Deities were created in both: there were three single deities and then several divine couples. The *Nihonshoki* states that the first three gods that were pure male showed up like a reed that connected earth to heaven.

A universal foundation was created for all the drifting cosmos, and then sand and mud collected on top of it. A pole was driven into it, and an inhabitable place was finally created.

The goddess Izanami and the god Izanagi showed up. They were ordered by their superiors who lived in heaven to create solid land from the materials drifting in the ocean. They were told to stand on a floating bridge in the heavens and stir the sea with a spear. They pulled the spear up to see if anything had gathered on the tip. When the salty water dripped off the end, it created the island called Onogoro. This island turned solid instantly. Izanami and Izanagi then came down to live on this island. They circled around a celestial pillar and met each other for the first time. They found each other sexually appealing and started producing things. After a few failures, they created the eight islands that makeup Japan.

They then created goddesses and gods of the winds, streams, valleys, mountains, trees, and many other of Japan's natural features. While Izanami was giving birth to Kagutsuchi, the fire god, she was severely burned. While she was dying, she created more goddesses and gods. These goddesses and gods presided over agriculture, earth, and metal. Other deities came from her husband's tears.

Izanagi was filled with anger at losing Izanami that he attacked Kagutsuchi. His blood created the god of thunder and other deities. In his grief, Izanagi went after Izanami to Yomi-tsu Kuni, which is a world of death and darkness that is considered to be the underworld, and pleaded with her to come back with him. She told him that she had already eaten food cooked on Yomi's stove and couldn't come back. Izanami was hiding in the shadows so that Izanagi couldn't see her. She asked him not to look at her, but Izanagi lit a torch and saw that she was covered in maggots and had already begun to decay, and he fled in terror. This made Iaznami feel humiliated and angry; she sent hideous spirits after him and chased him out of the underworld. Once he reached the upper world, he blocked the underworld's entrance with a huge stone. Izanami threatened Izanagi by telling him that she would kill 1000 people daily. He said that he would father 1500 children for each 1000 she killed. Izanami stayed in Yomi and ruled the dead.

Izanagi returned to his world and purified himself of the stench from Yomi by bathing in a stream. As he was undressing, goddesses and gods appeared from his clothing. While he was cleansing himself, the water that fell out of his left eye created Amaterasu Omikami, the sun goddess. She became the Imperial Family's ancestress. She is the best-known deity. She is responsible for fertility and brings light to the world. She has a shrine at Ise, and it is the most important shrine in all of Japan.

Amaterasu has two brothers who were formed from water that fell from Izanagi's right eye and nose. Tsukuyomi no Mikoto, the moon god, was formed from the water that fell from Izanagi's right eye, and Susanoo was formed from the water that fell from his nose. Tsu-kiyomi is the moon god, and Susanoo is a violent and powerful god who has been associated with storms. Susanoo has a more critical role in Japanese mythology as he has appeared in several significant legends, including many with Amaterasu. He is also known to be a trickster.

- Myths of Amaterasu

One myth speaks of how Susanoo was not happy with his share and caused a lot of destruction. He was soon banished to Yomi-tsu Kuni. He asked if he could go to heaven to visit his sister one more time. Amaterasu was worried that Susanoo would try to take over the sky, so she asked if he would participate in a contest.

He agreed to the contest that would prove their powers. If Susanoo won, he could remain heaven bit if he lost, he would have to go back to Yomi.

Amaterasu asked her brother for his sword. She broke this into three pieces and chewed on it. When she spits out the elements, they all turned into goddesses. Susanoo took a string of beads that were shaped like stars that Amaterasu had given to him. He chewed on the beads and spat out five gods. He claimed victory since he had created five gods, and Amaterasu had only created three goddesses. Amaterasu showed Susanoo that he had actually made gods from her possessions; this proved her power was more significant than his. Susanoo would not acknowledge defeat, and she allowed him to stay.

Susanoo soon became complacent with his success and started being a trickster. He did things that violated important taboos and offended his sister. He flung excrement all over Amaterasu's dining room when she was celebrating the first fruit's ceremony. He destroyed fields of rice, made horribly loud noises, and kept the floors of her palace filthy. Susanoo killed one of heaven's horses, skinned it, and hurled it into a hall where she was weaving cloth.

Amaterasu was enraged with his pranks, and she hid in a celestial cave and would not come out. When she concealed herself, soon darkness covered the earth and heavens. The plants stopped growing, and everything came to a screeching halt. The gods didn't know what to do, so 800 of them finally gathered to talk about ways to get her out of the cave. One god called Omori-Kane came up with a solution. The gods gathered at the entrance to the cave and hung a mirror on a branch of a tree that grew outside the cave. A young goddess,

Amemouzume, no Mikoto, danced half-naked. The gods laughed and applauded loudly. Amaterasu heard the commotion and wondered what was happening outside the cave. She opened the cave's door a bit and asked why they were happy. They lied to her and said they were celebrating because they found a goddess who was better than her. She became curious as to who that could be, and she opened the door a bit wider. She saw her image in the mirror. When she paused to look at herself, a god who was hiding close by pulled her out of the cave. Another god blocked the cave's entrance with a magical rope. When Amaterasu came out of the cave, her light began shining, and life returned. The gods banished Susanoo from heaven as punishment for all the problems he had caused.

- The Izumo Cycle

Soon the Izumo Cycle myths started to appear in the stories, and Okuninushi was the main character in these myths. Since he had angered the gods of heaven, Susanoo was banished from heaven. He descended to Izumo, where he rescued Kishiinada Hime or the Princess Marvellous Rice Field from a serpent with eight heads. He married the princess and became the forefather of the Izumo, a ruling family. The member of his family that was the most important was Okuninushi no Mikoto or the excellent earth chief. He controlled this region before the descendants of the sun goddess came to earth.

One of the more famous stories is about the White Rabbit. This tale goes something like this: Okuninushi had 80 brothers, and all of them wanted to marry the same princess. On one journey to see this princess, the guys found a rabbit without any fur in a lot of pain beside the road. They tricked the animal by telling it that it could get its coat back by bathing in some saltwater. This just made the rabbit's pain worse. Okuninushi came upon the rabbit a little time later. He asked the rabbit what had happened to him; the rabbit told him the tale of how he lost his fur.

The rabbit had been traveling between two islands, and he asked some crocodiles to create a bridge to the rabbit could cross without getting wet. In return for this, the rabbit has promised he would count the crocodiles to see if there were more of them than all the creatures in the sea. As the rabbit got closer to the shore, the crocodiles realized that his promise was just a trick to get to the other shore. The last crocodile got mad and grabbed the rabbit and tore off its fur. When Okuninushi heard his story, he told the rabbit to take a bath in clear water and then roll around in the grass pollen that had fallen to the ground. The rabbit did as directed, and new white fur soon began growing on his body. This rabbit was a god, and he rewarded Okuninushi by telling him that he could marry the beautiful princess. Okuninishi's success made his brothers angry, and there are several more myths about all the struggles between them.

- A Divine Emperor

It wasn't long before Amaterasu asked Okuninushi to give her the land of Izumo. She felt like "the land of the plentiful reed-covered plains and fresh rice ears" should be governed by her descendants. Once Izumo was given to her, she had Ninigi no Mikoto, her grandson, come to earth. It states in the *Nihonshoki* that Amaterasu gave Ninigi some rice ears from the sacred rice field and told him to plant rice on land while worshipping the celestial gods. She also gave him the mirror that was used to get her out of the cave, along with some jewels and the sword that belonged to Susanoo. He then came to earth and landed on Mount Fuji. He married one of the mountain god's daughters, whose name was Konohana-Sakuya Hime. With the treasures that he was sent to earth with, everyone accepted him as Japan's rules, and these treasures became the Imperial Family treasures.

Once his wife got pregnant and was going into labor, all in one night, he wanted proof that the child was really his. She set her room on fire and gave birth to three sons. One son became the father of Jimmu Tenno, the first emperor. He marked the time in history between the chronological age and the "age of the gods." His conquest of the Japanese heartland and eastern expedition was just a myth.

- Hachiman

The most popular deity in Japanese mythology is Hachiman. He was the patron of warriors. Hachiman's character was based on Ohin, the emperor, who lived in the 300s, and we are known for his military skills. According to legend, when Ojin died, he turned into the god Hachiman. He became part of the Shinto pantheon.

- Inari

There is a god called Inari who appears in some of the myths. He is important because he is associated with growing rice, which is Japans' major food crop. Inari was thought to bring them prosperity and is the patron of sword makers and merchants.

Spirits and Other Creatures

There are many creatures and spirits in Japanese mythology called the tengu. These are minor deities who are part bird and part human. They live in the mountainous regions and reside in trees there. They love playing tricks on humans but don't like being tricked. They aren't as wicked as they are mischievous.

One threatening group of spirits is called the Oni. They originated in China and traveled to Japan with Buddhism. These are horned demons and are usually huge in size. They can take on an animal or human shape. They are sometimes invisible, and they can steal human souls. They can be cruel and have been associated with evil forces like disease and famine.

This mythology includes other deities from Buddhism, too. Other than the stories about Buddha, there are several tales about Amida, who was the ruler of Pure Land, which was paradise. The protector of women in childbirth and children was known as Kannon. Jizo rescues souls from hell are other important figures in Buddhism.

Major Themes and Myths

The stories that are most important to Japanese myths deal with the goddess Amaterasu and creation. These are deeply rooted in nature, and they describe in detail how the lands were formed and the origins of light, wind, and fire.

As stated above, in the *Kojiki,* there was just ooze that the earth and heavens formed out of. Life soon emerged out of this ooze. There were three deities in heaven, and soon two more appeared. These five deities became the "Separate Heavenly Deities." They were quickly followed by the "Seven Generations of the Age of the Gods," which were made up of five male and female couples and two single deities. The two single gods came from a reed that was floating in the ooze.

Magical Creatures

There is a group of creatures that look like monkeys that are called the kappa. They display both evil and good qualities within the Japanese myths. They have been associated with water, and they live in lakes, ponds, and rivers. They carry water in a hollow spot at the top of their head. If water spills, they lose their magical powers. Kappas drink the blood of cattle, horses, and humans. They will also eat cucumbers. It is said that families could avoid getting attacked by them by throwing cucumbers that have their names on them into their watery homes.

The kappas do have some good qualities as they are very polite. When they meet anyone, they will bow, which usually causes them to spill the water from their heads. They also keep whatever promise they made. In most myths, humans can outwit kappa by making them make promises.

The Legacy of Japan's Mythology

Mythology still plays a massive role in the lives of the Japanese. Legends and myths are the basis of most of their literature, drama, and art. People are still learning and telling stories about these goddesses and gods. Their kagura dances are done to honor the deities of the Shinto shrine. Legend has traced the origin of this art form to the dance that got Amaterasu out of her cave.

CHAPTER 2

Japanese Kamis

Within the Shinto religion, the word kami is a term that can mean supernatural powers, natural phenomena, ancestors, deified mortals, spirits, and gods. All of these could influence a person's life daily, and so they get worshipped, asked for help, and given offerings. There were some cases when they were even appealed to for their divination shills. Kami gets attracted to purity, both the spiritual and the physical, and they get repelled by not enough of it, and this includes any and all disharmony. Kami has been associated with nature and might be present at places like unusually shaped rocks, trees, waterfalls, and mountains. Because of this, there are about eight million kami. Most kami are known throughout the nation, but many belong to just a small community. Every family will have its own ancestry of kami.

People being reverent to spirits that live in places of beauty, individual animals, and meteorological phenomena date back to about the first millennium BCE.

If you add all of these to the Shinto gods, family ancestors, and heroes along with the bodhisattvas that came from Buddhism and you have a limitless number of kami. There is one thing that is common with all kami are the four natures or spirits. One of these might be stronger depending on the circumstances: sakimitama means nurturing, kushimatama means wonderous, nigimitama means life- supporting or gentle, and aramitama or rough or wild. These divisions show that kami are capable of both evil and good. In spite of their huge numbers, kami could be put into other categories. There are various approaches to these categorizations. Some scholars will use kami's function while others use their nature. To make it simpler, since the ones mentioned usually overlap a lot.

Classical Kami

Classical kami are the ones that appear in the oldest texts like the *Nihonshoki* and the *Kojiki*. In this, you will find the gods. The most supreme among them is Amaterasu. Others will include her brother Susanoo, Okuninushi, Takamimusubi, and the gods of creation Izanagi and Izanami. The gods who stayed in the heavens are usually called amatsukami or heavenly kami.

In contrast, the next generation of gods ruled on earth first is known as kunitsukami or earthly kami. All kami in times of crisis will gather for a conference on the Heavenly River dried riverbed. Most important rocks, caves, mountains, and rivers will have their own kami. There are also two kami who come from across the sea, and they are Sarutahiko and Kukunabikona.

Later Kami

The next group of kami is the ones who were recognized after the early works had been written. This isn't saying that they weren't worshipped at a previous time. In this group, we have Hachiman. He was the god of culture and war. Inari, who was the commerce and rice god, is also in this group. The Japanese Emperor, who is reigning, is also considered to be a living kami. Any phenomena like wind, rain, and sunshine could be kami. The most famous is the divine wind or kamikaze that blew against the Mongol fleet that was invading Japan during the 13th century CE. Some people have been worshipped after their death. Some of these are former emperors, Tenman Tenjin, and the founder of the Tokugawa shogunal dynasty, Tokugawa Ieyasu. Some foreign gods have been accepted as kami. The most notable are Indra and Brahma, the Hindu gods, and Kannon, the Buddhist god. There are also "Seven Lucky Gods" or the schichifukujin: Jurojin, Hotei, Fukurokuju, Ebisu, Daikoku, Bishamon, and Benten. These are a mixed group of Japanese, Buddhist, Hindu, and Chinese gods, and they are a great example of the way Shinto has transformed, absorbed, and welcomed foreign deities into their large pantheon of kami.

Local Kami

The next group is the local kami. Even though many of these are generic kinds that have been recognized as powerful all through Japan, there is Ryujin or dragon kami, who is the kami of boundaries and crossroads. There are also kami of individual families, villages, and prominent local natural features. There might be times when white animals are given a kami. Most local kami will appear in pairs that will always be one female and one male.

Worshipping Kami

Kami is appeased, nourished, and appealed to try to make sure their influence is and will stay positive. Offerings like prayers, flowers, foods, and rice wine could help you reach this goal.

Music, dancing, rituals, and festivals can do this too. Shrines from huge complexes to simple affairs have been built to honor them. Each year, the object or image that is thought to be a physical manifestation of the kami gets taken through the community to purify it and to make sure of its well-being. The kami that was thought to be embodied by a natural feature was Mount Fuji. This is the best example and gets visited by worshippers as a way to pay homage.

Kami versus God

If the English word "god" gets translated into Japanese, it is usually represented by the kanji character and is pronounced kami. To not misunderstand, it would be best to think of "god," "kanji," and "kami" as three separate things.

"God" is usually the supreme omnipresent being that gets capitalized to show the deity has a unique nature that draws a distinction with all the other gods of all the different religions.

Japan's kami was initially thought to be anthropomorphized natural phenomena. These include any of the kami that are in the Kojiki and the Nihonshoki, anything that possesses extraordinary qualities like the sea, rain, wind, moon, and sun, along with the kami that are worshipped at shrines. Other kami might include people, animals, small plants, trees, and large rocks. This is how they got defined during the 18th century by the Japanese scholars of the Motoori Norinaga. According to this, anything that inspired sensitivity and awe to a fleeting beauty would be a kami.

For the Japanese people who believe in this, their country is a land full of natural landscapes where kami can be found anywhere you turn. Basically, it is a kami no Kuni or country of kami. If you were to translate this phrase into English, it would be called "God's country." It could be easily misunderstood as a "fanatically nationalistic expression," but this isn't what this phrase means.

Blended Faith

Japan's faith that is based on worshipping kami is called Shinto. There aren't any records that show what life was like during ancient times, and most of these details aren't clear. We can't say if there were any rituals or beliefs that could be called Shinto.

It is possible that this religion came about as a blend of various elements, including:

- Worshipping of family gods and then building shrines by the local groups and communities
- The influence of funeral rituals and festivals from Chinese thinkings, calendar studies, astronomy, and divination that are related to the legendary figures that are called "divine immortals."
- The bronze mirrors and weapons that were brought from China and used in magic rituals and festivals by their chiefs
- Worshipping clay figurines as the symbol for crop fertility and all the shamanism that was introduced from the Yayoi Period in the Korean Peninsula once rice farming became prevalent
- Hunter-gatherers worshipped nature during the Jomon period

The Japanese started thinking about these elements together as "Shinto" when Buddhism came into Japan. They then compared this new religion with their everyday practices.

Buddhas and Kami

Buddhism was formed in India by Gautama Buddha. He was born in either the 5th or 6th century BC. There have been many stories written about Buddha that includes a complex set of doctrines. Before it came to Japan, it was changed on its journey throughout China, where all the numerous texts were translated, and religious orders were organized and done in Chinese fashion. The Japanese developed their kami by contrasting them with the Buddhas. The main differences are:

- Buddhists create statues and likenesses of Buddhas and put them in temples, but the Buddha doesn't live in these temples. Believers of Shinto don't make likenesses of kami. Objects to attract kami are called yorishiro. They get put on shrines, but kami don't live in these shrines.
- Buddhas are always men, but they won't ever marry. Kami could either be female or male, and they will sometimes get married.
- Buddhas are living humans who have reached the most excellent enlightenment. When a Buddha dies, they have finally escaped from the cycle of death and life, and they no longer exist. Kami is different than ordinary humans. Some kami are ancestors of humans and could either die or live.

Along with other types of advanced Chinese culture like the ritsuryo system of architecture, medicine, calendar studies, astronomy, and centralized government, Buddha was a tool that the ruling class used to secure its prestige and power. After introducing these new beliefs, Shinto and Buddhism started occupying different spaces in the Japanese religion.

The Appeal of Buddhism and the Reform of Shinto

The Yamato Court began about the 3rd century AD in what is now known as the Kansai region. This was a confederation of all the forces throughout the region. They believed the only clan who were qualified to perform rituals were the descendants of Amaterasu. The people in other areas looked to various ancestors like the people who lived in Izumo worshipped Okuninushi. Myths about the harmonious existence of the various kami supported forming a confederation.

During the 8th century, the Kojiki and the Nihonshoki were finished. These compilations about the history and legends put Amaterasu as the most influential kami, and all the emperors were her descendants. These are the only people who can inherit the right to do rituals. Because of this, any forces outside of the imperial line lost all of these rights. The Yamato government didn't look at it this way and set up a "one god" religion just like the people of Israel did when they declared Yahweh to be the only true God. Rather, and this gave them the positions of hierarchy that was under Amaterasu. She has the cooperation between all the other kami, and this reinforced the collaboration between various groups.

By looking at it this way, Buddhas were notable because they were completely separated from the kami. This means they didn't have to be subordinate to Amaterasu. Anyone who had been excluded from the emperor's monopoly about power and ritual after the reform of Shinto could adopt Buddhism if they chose to do so. All of these forces were found around and in Yamato Province, which is now Nara Prefecture. By inheriting a bureaucratic government, they had developed into an aristocracy. Many of them embraced Buddhism. They built temples and hoped to be born again in the Western Paradise. The thought of being reincarnated as a Buddha after one died was very different from the Shinto tenets. In contrast, any of the peasants who worked at any of the estates that belonged to the aristocracy, shrines, and temples, their faith in local kami was more natural and familiar than Buddhism.

Various Ideas about Death and Life

How did the Japanese view the afterworld? Well, some thought that their soul would return to the mountain. Others believed that they would go underground to the land of death known as Yoni. While others thought they would cross the sea into a paradise that was called Tokoyo. Some people believed in defilement that was associated with death, and the dead traveled far from where living people lived.

Every Emperor worshipped Amaterasu, other kami, and their own ancestors. All the religious ceremonies were based on the Chinese models but honoring their deceased ancestors was only found in Japan. It was thought that the dead emperors turned into kami after their defilement had been cleansed in someplace that was very far away.

In contrast, Buddhism says that people have to work to attain nirvana by doing ascetic practices while going through the cycle of life and into death. If a person died without reaching nirvana, they were immediately reincarnated into new bodies to start their lives repeatedly. They didn't believe in the land of the dead, and people didn't have an eternal soul. Basically, original Shinto and Buddhism have entirely different ideas about death.

The idea of reincarnation wasn't immediately accepted in Japan when Buddhism was brought into their country. The Chinese belief that dead people turn into demons that lived in hell came into Japan through Taoism, and Buddhism began spreading slowly. Buddhism got more popular when it changed its views to those that were accepted by the people of Japan.

Meet the Gods

The following kami come from both the Japanese Buddhist and Shinto traditions. Most have been influenced by Chinese, Indian, Roman, and Greek goddesses and gods.

- Jizo

This is the guardian of childbirth and children.

The ancient Japanese thought that children who died before their parents couldn't cross the Sanzu River into the afterlife since they hadn't lived long enough to accumulate enough good deeds. They were doomed to stand on the shore of the river and stack small rocks.

The god Jizo helps these children cross the river. He does this by hiding them in his robe. Any statue you see of Jizo will be reasonably small. They usually appear in large numbers at temples all over Japan. There are over one million Jizo statues in this country. These are generally donated by the parents of dead children. Jizo is given hats and bibs to keep them warm. There will be some temples where you will find stacks of rocks or toys in front of the Jizo to ensure their child is safe during their afterlife.

- Fujin and Raijin

Fujin is the wind kami who is usually shown holding a bag full of wind. Raijin is the storm, thunder, and lightning kami. They are normally shown holding a hammer and surrounded by drums.

Fujin and Raijin usually appear together. They are feared a lot because of the damage that storms and typhoons have wreaked in Japan.

Parents would tell their children to make sure their bellybutton were hidden during a storm so that Raijin would eat their bellies.

Since these are feared deities, Fuijin and Raijin usually appear together at the gate to a shrine to protect it. Every visitor to these sacred places had to pass by the gaze of these deities who were so frightening.

- Ungaro and Agyo

Ungaro and Agyo are the Buddha's scary guardians who usually stand at the entrance to any temple in Japan.

Agyo is their symbol of violence. His statues show him baring his teeth and either him clenching his fists or holding weapons. Ungaro stands for strength. His mouth will always be shut, and he shows that his hands are empty as a sign of confidence.

- Inari

She is the goddess of all the things that are important to the Japanese culture like worldly success, sake, fertility, tea, and rice. Her earthly messengers are foxes. Because of this, foxes hold a lot of respect in Japan.

Most shrines in Japan will have small shrines to the side that have been dedicated to foxes. It is common to give the foxes an offering of aburaage. It is thought that foxes are crazy about this food. Most shrines will have some statues of foxes at them too.

- Kannon

She is the Buddhist goddess of mercy. She is considered to be a Bodhisattva or a person who has achieved enlightenment. She postponed her Buddhahood until everybody has been enlightened.

Most temples have been dedicated to worship her. She is also featured in the Japanese Christian imagery of the Edo-era.

During the 1600s, Japan banned Christianity. The Christians still worshiped in secrecy. These Christians made statues to honor Kannon that looked a lot like the Roman Catholic's Madonna and Child. They included some Christian symbols like crosses. Some figures have survived for many years and can be seen at some Japanese temples still today.

- Benzaiten

This goddess is also known as Benten. She is the goddess of everything that flows like music, eloquence, and words. She has also been associated with love. It is typical for any shrine that has been dedicated to her to be thought of as a romantic spot for couples. She is one of the Seven Lucky Gods.

The Enoshima Shrine that was dedicated to Benzaiten is very popular with couples because of its pink prayer boards with hearts.

- Ebisu or Yebisu

Yebisu is sometimes written as Ebisu. he was born without bones and struggled just to live. When he was two, he was put into the sea in a boat. He did survive, and he grew bones. He came back from the ocean several years later to be considered as a god.

He is the god of luck, fishermen, and he guards small children and the hearth. He is delighted even though he has had a rough life.

Yebisu is normally seen as a chubby guy wearing a hat and carrying a fishing rod with a fish. In more modern times, he has been known as the god on the Yebisu beer cans.

- Amaterasu

She is the goddess of the universe and sun. She has been considered as the most important Shinto god. The Emperor is thought to be a descendant of Amaterasu. This was emphasized during the years between 1868 to 1945 when Shinto was a government organization. When WWII was over, Emperor Showa made a statement over the radio that he did not consider himself as a kami.

- Shitenno

This translates to "Four Heavenly Kings." These are four gods who are terrifying and were borrowed from the Hindu to protect the Buddhist temples. Every god is associated with a specific element, virtue, season, or direction. In most cases, Shitenno is shown stomping on demons.

- Izanagi and Izanami

Izanami and Izanagi are the Shinto gods of creation. The created the earth by using a spear that had been decorated with jewels. They used this spear to stir the sea located between the earth and heaven. Every time a drop of water fell off the spear, it created an island.

- Tengu

This is a bird monster that can take on the form of a human. When they are in human form, they will have huge noses.

Tengu has always been thought of as the enemy of Buddhism who corrupted monks and their followers. In modern times, they have been viewed as the protectors of sacred mountains and forests.

Tengu isn't normally kami. They are generally considered to be ghosts or monsters. But, some temples that are located in sacred mountains and forests have been associated with tengu kami.

- Sugawara no Michizane

This kami was a prominent Japanese politician and poet who got exiled by his rivals in 901. He died a lonely man shortly after this.

Immediately after he died, Kyoto was struck with lots of floods and terrible lightning. All of the sons of the Emperor died in unusual accidents. Droughts and plague spread wildly through Japan.

The government said this was caused by Sugawara no Michizane's vengeful spirit. They restored his status and ranked posthumously. They tried to get rid of all the evidence of his punishment. When the disaster continued happening, they gave his spirit the title of Kami of Scholarship for special ceremonies. They built a shrine in Kyoto to honor him. It is called the Kitano Tenmangu Shrine. The disasters finally ended.

- Taira no Masakado

He was a samurai that challenged the Imperial court located in Kyoto. He took over large parts of Japan before he was defeated in battle in the year 940. They brought his head back to Tokyo, and he was enshrined at Kanda Shrine.

Taira no Masakado was very popular with the people since he challenged the government. There were rainbows, lunar eclipses, butterfly swarms, and earthquakes in Kyoto before his revolt.

He was considered to be a very powerful kami. He has to be appeased continuously, or bad luck will happen. He has been blamed for fires and floods in the Edo-era. The Shoguns would visit his shrine to pray for him.

CHAPTER 3

Mythology Terminology

Since the original stories were written in Japanese, some terminology can be a bit difficult to understand if you are not familiar with the Japanese language. On a similar note, their symbolism can be a bit different than what some are used to as well. To ensure you understand and appreciate the stories, we will go over some words and symbolism that you may find helpful.

Glossary

Aku – means evil, but the meaning does not only include moral evil, but also includes unhappiness, misfortune, and inferiority.

Anzen – it is a type of omamori, specifically for safety. Its primary purpose is safety at work and is often requested from a kami.

Aramitama – means wild soul, and refers to the violent and rough side of a complete spirit.

Bon Matsuri – a festival that is held around July 15th to help console the spirits of death. This is, in theory, a Buddhist festival. In practice, though, it is a family and ancestor festival part of Shinto.

Bunrei – the division process for a kami where it produces two copies of the original.

Chi – means intelligence, wisdom, and knowledge. It is one of the seven virtues.

Chochin – these are paper lanterns that are present at Shinto festivals.

Chugi – means loyalty and duty. It is one of the seven virtues.

Daijosai – this is a ceremony that marks the start of an Emperor's reign.

Dosojin – a group of kami that protects places of transition, roads, and borders.

Gi – means righteousness. It is one of the seven virtues.

Giri – means burden, duty, obligation, and responsibility. It is one of the seven virtues.

Goryo – an angry soul that is upset for having died unhappy or violently.

Haku – means vitalism, soul, and life force. It comes from Daoism and is a part of the soul that is indissolubly attached to the body and will return to the earth after the person dies.

Jin – means compassion and benevolence. It is one of the seven virtues.

Jisei – means self-restraint, temperance, and self-control. It is one of the seven virtues.

Kagura – means divine entertainment. It is also a type of Shinto dance that is connected to the Emperor and his family. It is also a dance performed at shrines during their religious rites.

Kakuriyo – it's literal meaning is a hidden world, which means either the spirits or kami or the world of the dead.

Kami – a term that broadly means deity or spirit, but also has many other meanings:

- Deities talked about in Japanese mythology and local gods who protect families, areas, and villages.
- Non-anthropomorphic spirits who are unnamed and are found in natural phenomena.
- A basic sense of sacred power.

The famous definition by Motoori Norinaga, "a kami is anything or phenomenon that produces the emotions of fear and awe, with no distinction between good and evil."

Kanjo – the process where a kami is transferred to a shrine.

Ko – means filial piety. It is one of the seven virtues.

Kon – means vitalism, soul, and life force. It comes from Daoism and is the part of the soul that can leave the body and go to heaven once a person dies. It carries with it the appearance of a physical form.

Kotodama – this is the supernatural power that words possess.

Makoto – means sincerity and honesty. It is one of the seven virtues.

Meiyo – means honor. It is one of the seven virtues.

Mitama – this is the soul of a dead person or the spirit of a kami.

Onryo – means vengeful spirit. It is a type of vengeful spirit; a poltergeist.

Rei – means etiquette, manners, and respect. It is one of the seven virtues.

Shintai – means a divine body. It is a sacred object, typically a sword, jewel, or mirror representing the kami for worship.

Tei – means fraternity. It is one of the seven virtues.

Torii – means bird perch. It is an iconic Shinto gate that is located at the entrance of scared spaces.

Toro – means a stone lamp case. It is a lantern place in a shrine or temple.

Ujigami – means clan deity. It is a guardian spirit or god of a particular area in the Shinto region.

Yu – means courage. It is one of the seven virtues.

Yurei – means dark spirit. It is a type of phantom or ghost.

Symbolism

The Blue Lotus – This is a symbol of wisdom and victory for the spirit over the senses. The lotus symbolizes enlightenment and purity, and in every Buddhist tradition, the deities are most often depicted standing or sitting atop a lotus or holding one. While the flower is beautiful, it is only able to be grown in the mud at the bottom of a pond. The Buddhist deities are enlightened beings who have grown out of the mud of the material world. An open blossom is representative of the possibility of universal salvation for sentient beings.

Mirror – The mirror brings forth intelligence to liberate the mind. It reflects the lesson that life is simply an illusion, for a mirror does not show us the reality. It is only a reflection of our existence. This makes the mirror a metaphor for the unenlightened mind that is concerned with mere appearances.

Bonsai Tree – The monks who brought the bonsai to Japan saw these trees as symbols for harmony between the soul, nature, and man. The tree also changes. The grotesque and bizarre shapes of fierce dragons and serpents were gone. Life in their place was balance, harmony, and peace. The bonsai tree then became a representation of all that was good.

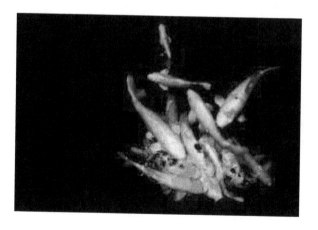

Koi Fish – The koi fish represents luck or good fortune, but they are also connected to perseverance in adversity and the strength of purpose. It represents courage in Buddhism. Today, these fish are seen as the advancement of spirituality and materials.

Butterflies – The butterfly represents the soul of the living and dead. They are seen as symbols of longevity and joy.

Cranes – This bird also represents good fortune and longevity. They are closely connected to the Japanese New Year, as well as wedding ceremonies. They will often be woven into a wedding obi or kimono.

CHAPTER 4

Amaterasu and The Cave

"There are quite a few stories out there about the sun taking a vacation for one reason or another, and they rarely end well for anybody. The sun is crucial for us humans, as we need it to live. When it decides to take a little trip, people often object because we may die. But that is where we find ourselves with the story of Amaterasu.

Amaterasu was the oldest daughter of Izanagi and Izanami, the creators of Earth. The pair had worked together to form every piece of land on Earth, from the

mountains that rose high into the sky to the waters that rippled around the land. After they had formed the Earth, Izanagi and Izanami wished to form a life that could folic upon their creation. They then gave birth to Amaterasu, who's beauty and radiance brought joy to her parents. They placed her high in the sky where everybody could see, and she protected the day in the form of the sun.

Soon after, Amaterasu had two siblings. The god of the moon, Tsuki-Yomi, who was very composed and peaceful and was only a fraction as bright as Amaterasu. The god of the seas, Susanoo, who was a boy with a horrible temperament who was very prone to violent action. Susanoo's rage and love of causing problems in the ocean eventually caused him to be demoted as the god of the underworld, but that is a different story for another day.

As you could suspect, Susanoo was not happy about having to be in the underworld. One day, as he was taking in some of Amaterasu's rays and taking a break from the underworld, he gets an idea. He approached Amaterasu with a proposition. Amaterasu was a bit reluctant, given Sunsanoo's temper. She relented and listened to his proposition. He suggested that they play a game of God making, but they didn't make their rule clears. At the end of the game, they have successfully formed eight new Gods, and they both declared themselves a winner. As Susanoo got more enraged, Amaterasu left him to cool off.

She headed to her weaving room to work on a project. As Amaterasu was weaving on her loom, there came an offensive attack from her brother. Infuriated by how beloved and beautiful she was, Susanoo killed her mare and tossed it into the weaving room. It ruined all of the looms and the project she was working on. It's believed that Susanoo's rage was so great that he killed an attendant girl in the room and even attacked Amaterasu, which caused the gentle goddess to flee from her palace.

Amaterasu sought refuge in a cave in a mountain, refusing to shine any light or joy upon the world. The longer she hid in the cave, the Earth started to wither and die. This caused demons to start crawling out of the underworld and wreaking their own chaos upon the animals, people, and plants on the surface of the Earth.

Knowing that the world was not looking so good, the Gods and Goddesses came together outside of the cave and tried to lure Amaterasu out of the cave to shine her light on the Earth again. The Gods and Goddesses didn't do a good job at coming up with a plan to get her out.

Their first attempt was to place a bunch of roosters outside of the cave. They hoped that if Amaterasu heard all of their crowings, she would think that it was time for the sun to rise and come out. As you would expect, this plan didn't work so well.

Then they came up with a plan using a mirror. They placed a huge mirror facing into the cave Amaterasu was in and leaned it against a nearby rock. They hung jewels from the trees and started to dance around, urging all of the other Gods and Goddesses to join in. They had hoped that their festivities would intrigue the sun Goddess so much that she couldn't help but ask what was going on. To which they would reply with, 'We have found a new much better sun goddess!'

They would then cause Amaterasu to look outside of the cave and see what all of the commotions were about. When she did, Amaterasu saw her own reflection in the mirror. She was hypnotized by her own beauty, causing her to leave the cave.

Alas, this did not work out as planned. That's when the Goddess Uzume came forward. She is the Goddess of the arts, revelry, meditation, joy, and dawn. She suggested that the best way to get Amaterasu out of her cave would be with dance. Since she is Goddess of partying and fun, she had no problem with doing a dance for Amaterasu, if it means that it could save the world.

The dancing got Amaterasu's attention, and she peeked her head out of the cave. When she did this, she saw the roosters, the mirror, and the enthusiastic dancing goddess. She actually left the cave this time. It was just Uzume, but all three things working together to draw her out and distract her from her anger. After she stepped back outside, a giant rock was placed in front of the cave to prevent her from hiding away again. She soon found herself immersed in the amusement of her family and friends.

Unable to remain upset and frowning about her misfortune, Amaterasu let her light shine upon the Earth again. As soon as the world was filled with her light once more, the disease and demons set upon the land receded into the Underworld. Susanoo gets banished from the heavens for causing this problem. He would wander the Earth for awhile having adventures until he eventually he can get back into the good graces of Amaterasu by giving her the legendary sword, Grass-Cutter."

CHAPTER 5

The One-Inch Boy – Issun-Boshi

"A long time ago in a Japanese village, there lived an old man and his wife, who more than anything, wanted to have a child. They constantly hoped and wished for the child. They would go to the temple and pray to the gods. 'May we be blessed with a child,' they would say, 'even if he is no larger than our thumbs.'

One day, they finally got the answer to their prayers. Outside their home, they could hear baby cries. The old couple looked at each other and said, 'Perhaps the great Buddha has answered our prayer at last.' He eased the door open and resting on the step was a tiny baby. The child was quite lovely, and he was little. They named the boy Issun Boshi, which meant *One-Inch Boy*, for he wasn't any taller than his father's thumb.

While Issun Boshi never grew any bigger, he did grow up to be helpful, healthy, and smart. He had the heart of a lion, and while his parent's small garden had been a constant source of adventure for the small boy, his great ambition was to become a Samurai and serve a Lord in Kyoto. When Issun Boshi turned 12 years old, he went to his parents and said, 'Father and Mother, please give me your permission to go to the capital city, for I wish to see the world, learn many things, and make a name for myself.'

His parents were distraught and scared when they thought about all of the bad things that could happen to Issun Boshi is such a big city, but they also knew that their boy was strong and smart, so they said that he could go. They created a tiny sword for him using a sewing needle. They also gave him a rice bowl that he could use as a boat and some chopsticks to use as oars.

As he floated down the river in his rice bowl boat, he used the chopsticks as his paddles whenever the water turned rough, and he would use his sword to catch fish. After a few days, he made it to the city of Kyoto. 'My, what a busy city this is!' he thought to himself. 'So many people crammed into one space!' He carefully walked through the streets and dodged cartwheels and feet. He continued to walk until he came to a beautiful. It was the largest house in the city. At the bottom of the stairs sat a pair of shiny black geta, or wooden shoes. They were the owners of the house, who was the wealthiest lord in the city. This was the home of the famous Lord Sanjo.

The door to the large house opened. Out walked a man who put on the shiny black shoes that Issun Boshi has seen. The little boy called out, 'Hello! Hello up there!' The man quickly looked down and around, and when he saw no one, he started to go back inside. Issun Boshi called out once more, 'Down here! I'm down here, near your shoes! Please be careful you don't step on me.' The man, who was the lord of the house, bent down and was amazed to find the small boy. Issun Boshi bowed and politely introduced himself. 'My name,' he started, 'is Issun Boshi. I have just arrived in the city, and I would like to work for you.'

The lord picked up the small boy and sat him in the palm of his hand. In a pleasant voice, the man asked, 'But what can a fellow like you do?'

Issun Boshi had noticed a little fly buzzing around the head of the lord and bother him. Issun Boshi draws out his makeshift sword and, with a quick swat, away went the fly.

'You are quite an amazing little fellow,' laughed the lord. 'Come, you may work for me and live in my house.'

And so, tiny Issun Boshi went to live in a large, beautiful house and served the noble lord. He quickly became friends with everybody that lived there, especially the princess, the daughter of the lord. It seemed as though she was always by his side, helping her in whatever way he was able to. This could be holding down the paper she was writing on, or only by riding on her shoulder and keeping her company while she walked through the gardens of the beautiful house. After some time, the princess started to form strong affection for her little helper.

During the spring, Issun Boshi traveled with the princess and her companion to visit the cherry blossom festival. While they are traveling back home, they start to hear some odd noises behind them on the narrow road. They could not see nothing in the shadows when suddenly, a gigantic monster leaped into their path.

Everybody in the group ran and screamed, that is, everybody except for Issun Boshi and the princess.

'Who are you, and what do you want?' screamed Issun Boshi.

'I am an oni,' growled the monster.

An oni! The oni was very terrible creatures, who liked to bother and torment the townspeople. But Issun Boshi stepped forward and shouted once more, saying, 'Get out of the way, you demon! I am here to guard the princess. Step back!'

'Ha! We'll see about that!' growled the oni. He snatched up Issun Boshi. 'You are no bigger than a mouse, and a small one at that.' The oni popped him in his mouth, and with a single gulp, he swallowed him whole. Down, down, down, Issun Boshi slid until he plopped into the oni's stomach.

'This oni should be more careful about what he eats,' said Issun Boshi. He pulled out his makeshift sword and started tickling the oni's stomach.

'Ow! Ooh! Agh!' shouted the oni. Shortly, the oni gave out a loud burp, and out came Issun Boshi. The oni ran away, burping the whole way.

Issun Boshi raced back over to the princess. She bent down and picked something up off of the ground. With much excitement, she said, 'Look, Issun Boshi, the oni was so scared he dropped his magic hammer. If you make a wish on it, it will come true.'

Issun Boshi bowed to the princess and replied, 'My lady, I would ask that you make a wish.'

'No, Issun Boshi,' said the princess, 'You won this because of your bravery. You should be the first one to wish on it.'

With that, Issun Boshi took the hammer and said, 'I already have my greatest wish, which is to serve you, but if I could have another wish, I would wish to be as tall as other people.'

He then handed the hammer to the princess, who made a silent wish on it herself. Then and there, Issun Boshi felt himself start to grow taller. He continued to grow until he stood beside the princess, a handsome young man.

That night, after the princess told her father about how brave Issun Boshi had been, and he had risked himself to save her, the lord was so happy that he allowed Issun Boshi to marry the princess. With that, the princess's wish came true, too.

Issun Boshi's brave deeds were celebrated across the land. He and the princess would live happily together, along with Issun Boshi's proud and happy parents, whom Issun Boshi brought to the lord's house to join his new family. From that day on, he became known as General Horikawa, a handsome and gallant Samurai."

CHAPTER 6

Susanoo and Orochi

"Poor Susanoo. There was nobody in the heavens who liked him because of all the problems he caused. Nobody even wanted to be close to him. But was it really his fault that, as the tempest God, he was always accompanied by a flurry of stormy destruction no matter where he went? Was it really his fault that his name meant impetuous males? Which was a title that was not so easy to warm up to or even appreciate?

And then there was that whole incident with the horse. Susanoo really didn't have a clue as to why his dear sister got so upset. It was nothing more than a bit of rowdy fun between siblings.

But nobody saw things the same way that he did, as usual. Everybody, he felt, was always overreacting. As his dear sister emerged out of the cava, Susanoo was banished from the heavens. Before he was banished, he acquired silkworms, soybeans, azuki, wheat, millet, and rice. In a pretty foul mood, as would be expected, he wandered the province of Izumo, doing his best not to cause too many problems for the local ecology with the storm clouds that were still following him.

He reached a river when he noticed a pair of chopsticks floating downstream. With that, he chose to travel upstream in hopes of finding some local residents.

It wasn't long before his wandering brought him before an elderly couple who were crying in the wilderness. After a little bit of convincing, the two aged ones told Susanoo, between sobs, that seven of their eight daughters had been eaten by a monstrous eight-headed snake called Yamata-no-Orochi. Orochi came every year and would eat one of their daughters. They bemoaned that their last daughter would soon befall the same grisly fate.

They described the dragon as having blazing bloodshot eyes, eight tails, and eight heads attached to a gigantic body that spanned across eight mounts and eight valleys. On the back of the dragon grew moss, cypresses, and birches. His underbelly was inflamed and oozed blood and pus.

'I could help you out, you know,' Susanoo casually said after the couple had finished with their story. 'I am the God of Storms, after all. Even a 100-headed serpent wouldn't be a match for me. However, in order for me to help you, you must promise me a reward. Let's say, your remaining daughter? If I kill the snake, I get to keep her as my wife.'

'You're joking,' the elderly man gasped in horror. 'You're just someone who walked out of the forest claiming to be a god. You expect us to hand over our last daughter because of your verbal claim?'

'Hey, nobody's forcing you to do anything, and I am not asking for her hand in marriage now. We only get married after I have killed the eight-headed serpent.'

'But you're a god!' the elderly woman cried, 'Shouldn't you be rescuing people for free?'

'Lady, if you were a goddess, would you rescue people for free? Now, do we have a deal, or do we now?'

The three of them sat and negotiated for a long time, with the elderly couple ultimately agreeing out of complete and utter desperation. Happy with how things had turned out, Susanoo planned out what he would do next. 'How should I do this?' He mused as the elderly couple glared. 'Zap it with lightning? Summon a massive flood to drown it? Wait, wait! I should rain flayed horses on its heads. Now that would be fun…'

After some time, he eventually decides to approach the fight with a combination of wit, magic, and raw might. Only at that point would it befit his status as the might Shinto God of storms and impress the hearts of the humans.

The first step of his plan meant he had to transform Kushinada-Hime, the last daughter, into a comb and placed her in his hair to keep her safe. Since he was a storm god, his mane of hair was always perfectly disheveled chaos at all times.

Then he instructed that a hedge should be built that encircled a large field. It was to have eight separate gates built into it.

Next, he told the couple to brew up enough sake to fill eight large tubs and to place those tubes around the wilderness for Orochi to find and drink. Specifically, one tube for each hand. With the brewing skills of the couple, and everything else proceeding as he had planned, it wouldn't be long before the serpent would be drunk.

Susanoo sheltered away, waiting for Orochi to arrive. Suddenly, ominous filled the area. Dark, eerie clouds feel around the place, with thunder and lightning following. They were soon in the midst of a storm. The land was rocked by massive tremors. The hills around them crumbled before their very eyes, and trees were mowed down, making horrible sounds. Then the monster was before them. His breaths turned into windstorms.

For some time, Orochi stood there and sniffed the air. Lured by the sweet smell of the sake, Orochi began to drink all of the wine greedily. Each head was taking care of their own vat. It wasn't long before he was drunk and sleeping in the middle of the hedge, snoring loudly.

After this, Susanoo crept to the serpent and effortlessly lopped off every head using his massive sward. Just be on the safe side, he also diced up the body of the serpent. He felt that the meat would probably make for a pretty umai serpent sashimi during the wedding.

'What is this!' he shouted when his sword was suddenly stopped by something hard in the tail of the Orochi. When he checked his blade, he noticed a deep notch in it. Something deep within Orochi had been steely enough to dent the edge of this magical sword. Had it been his spine? Maybe Orochi had eaten some ore? No, that couldn't be it. Who would believe it? After he sliced away the remainder of his flesh, Susanoo found a magnificent sword embedded within the tail of Orochi. One glance at this deadly blade and Susanoo knew the sword had no equal existence. With his godly knowledge, Susanoo knew that this sword would be able to live on forever in myths and legends.

'Danna,' Kushinada-Hime whispered with worry in Susanoo's hair as he marveled at the blade. 'A sword in a dead snake. Is this an omen that you are going to be an abusive husband? Should I be worried and start looking for caves to hide in?'

'Nonsense, silly girl,' Susanoo grinned. 'This will ensure that we live on forever in the hearts of mortals near and far. Think about it. Who else would find a legendary weapon this way? Everybody else just shoots them from afar.'

And so it was as the God of Storms had predicted. The sword in the snake became known as Ame-no-Mura-kumo-no-Tsurugi and became one of the most famous swords in Japanese history. This was the sword Susanoo would ultimately give to his sister Amaterasu, who would gift the sword to the great Japanese warrior-emperor Yamato Takeru. Today, this legendary blade is revered as one of the Three Imperial Regalia of Japan. The existence of this blade represents the divine connection between the Japanese Royal Family and the Gods of Shinto. As Susanoo foresaw, the story of the incredible discovery continues to inspire many today.

After he defeated Orochi, Susanoo married Kushinada and settled into Izumo. Susanoo would compose a poem in honor of his new wife and the land of Izumo. This poem is considered to be the first *Waka* in recorded history."

CHAPTER 7

The Tongue-Cut Sparrow

"Many, many years ago in Japan, there lived an old man and his wife. The senior fellow was a hard-working, kind-hearted, and good older man, but that was the case for his wife. She was a regular crosspatch. She could spoil the happiness of her home simply through scolding. She was always fussing about something from day tonight. The old man had gotten used to her crossness and didn't even notice it anymore. He worked most of the days in the fields, and, since they had no children, for his amusement when he returned home, he took care of a tame sparrow. He cared about that little bird just as much as if she had been his child.

Each night, when he returned home after a hard day's work in the open air, it was his only pleasure to get to pet his sparrow, to talk with her, and to teach her some simple tricks, which she was able to pick up very quickly. He would open up her cage and allow her to fly around the room, and they would play for some time together. Once it was supper time, he would always save some bits from his plate that he would use to feed his little bird.

The Feast of Dolls. A Japanese Home on the Third Day of the Third Month. (Drawn by Nashoku Oasus.)

There was one day when the old man went out into the forest to chop some wood, and the old woman stopped at home to wash their clothes. The day before, she had mixed up some fresh starch, and now that she was look-ing for it, it was all gone. The bowl that had been filled full yesterday was completely empty. While she was trying to figure out who could have stolen or used all of the starch, down flew her husband's pet sparrow. She bowed her little feathered head, which she had been taught by her master, the pretty bird chirped and said, 'It is I who have taken the starch. I thought it was some food put out for me in that basin, and I ate it all.

If I have made a mistake, I beg you to forgive me! Tweet, tweet, tweet.'

You can see by the sparrow's actions that it was a truthful bird, and the older woman, if she had been a kindly woman, would have been willing to forgive her when she asked her pardon so nicely. But that is not what the old woman did.

The old woman had never cared for the sparrow and had fought with her husband on numerous occasions about keeping what she would often call a dirty bird about the house. She said that it only did extra work for her. Now she was only too happy to have something to complain about against the pet. She scolded and even cursed the poor little bird for the way she had acted, and not happy with just her hard, unfeeling words, in a fit of rage, she grabbed up the sparrow. The sparrow had remained with her wings spread out, and her head bowed before the old woman as she was scolded to show how sorry she was. Once the old woman had the sparrow in hand, she grabbed a pair of scissors and cut off the bird's tongue.

'I supposed you took my starch with that tongue! Now you may see what it is like to go without it!' With those words, she drove the birds away, not caring at all what would come of the bird and without the tiniest bit of pity for its suffering.

The old woman, once she had raced the sparrow away, mixed up some more rice-paste, grumbling the entire time about all of the trouble, and once she starched all of the clothes, she spread them out on boards to dry in the sun instead of ironing them.

Once the evening came, the old man made his way home. As was usual for him, on the way back, he looked forward to the time when he should get to the gate and see his pet come chirping to meet him, ruffling up her feathers to show her happiness before coming to land on his shoulder. Tonight, though, the old man was disappointed, for he didn't even see the shadow of his sparrow.

He picked up his pace, and hastily pulled off his straw sandals before stepping onto the veranda. Still, he could not see a sparrow. He felt for sure that his wife, in one of her cross tempers, had locked the sparrow up in its cage. He called out to her and said anxiously, 'Where is Suzume San today?'

The old woman decided to play dumb and pretend to not know what had happened, and replied with, 'Your sparrow? I am sure I don't know. Now I come to think of it, and I haven't seen her all that afternoon. I shouldn't wonder if the ungrateful bird had flown away and left you after all your petting!'

But the old man would not give his wife any peace on the subject. Instead, he would ask again and again where the bird was, insisting that she had to know what became of his pet. She finally confessed to what she had done. She told him crossly how the sparrow had eaten all of the rice- paste that she had made specifically for starching the clothes and how the sparrow had told her everything. Then she told him how, in great anger, she had taken scissors and cut out the bird's tongue, and how she had finally driven the bird away and forbade her to return to their house ever again.

She then pulled out the sparrow's tongue and said, 'Here is the tongue I cut off! Horrid little bird, why did it eat all of my starch?'

'How could you ever be so cruel? Oh, how could you be so cruel?' That was all that the old man could muster. He was too kind-hearted to punish his shrew of a wife but is extremely upset about what had been done to his poor little sparrow.

'What a dreadful misfortune for my poor Suzume San to lose her tongue!' he muttered to himself. 'She won't be able to chirp any more, and surely the pain of the cutting of it out in that rough way must have made her ill! Is there nothing to be done?'

Once his cross wife had fallen asleep for the night, the old man shed many tears. As he wiped away the tears with the sleeve of his robe, a bright thought came to him. He was going to go out and look for the sparrow on the morrow. Having made this choice, he finally could go to sleep.

The following morning he woke up early as soon as daylight broke. After he grabbed a quick breakfast, he started out over the hills and through the woods. He would stop at every single clump of bamboo to cry out, 'Where, oh where, does my tongue-cut sparrow stay? Where, oh where, does my tongue-cut sparrow stay?'

He didn't stop to rest for his lunch, and it was very late into the afternoon when he found himself near a large bamboo thicket. Bamboo groves are one of the most favorite places for sparrows, and sure enough, at the edge of the wood, he spotted his dear sparrow waiting to welcome him. He couldn't believe his eyes and ran straight for her to greet her. She bowed her little head and went through all of the tricks that she had been taught to show her happiness in getting to see her old friend again. To the old man's surprise, she could talk just like before.

The old man apologized to her and for what had happened and asked how she could speak so wonderfully without it. The sparrow opened up her beak and showed him that she had a new tongue that had grown in place of the old one. She begged him not to think about the past anymore, for she was quite well. The old man soon realized that his sparrow was a fairy and not a common bird. It would be hard to exaggerate how happy the man was right now. He forgot about all of his troubles. He even forgot about how tired he was, for he had finally found his beloved lost sparrow. Instead of being ill and without her tongue, as the old man had feared, she was happy and well with a brand new tongue. She had no sign of the ill-treatment she had received from his wife. Above all else, she was a fairy.

The sparrow asked the old man to follow her and to fly just in front of him, and she led him to a fantastic house in the center of the bamboo grove. The old man was utterly taken aback when he walked into the house. He found that it was a beautiful place. It had been built from the whitest of wood. The soft cream-colored mats, which were placed down in place of the carpets, were the nicest he had ever seen. The cushions that the sparrow brought to the man to sit upon were made of the finest silk and crape. Lacquer boxes and beautiful vases decorated the tokonoma of each room.

The sparrow took the old man to the place of honor, and then, taking her one spot at a humble distance, she thanked the old man with many polite bows for all of his kindness that he had given her for so many long years. Then, Lady Sparrow called in her family and introduced them to the old man.

After the introductions were finished, her daughters dressed in dainty crape gowns brought in a feast of delicious foods on old-fashioned trays. They brought in so much food that the old man thought he had to be dreaming. In the middle of their dinner, some of the sparrow's daughters performed a wonderful dance that is called the Suzume-Odori, or 'the Sparrow's dance,' to entertain the guest.

Never had the old man had so much fun? The hours flew by much too quickly in this lovely place with all of the fairy sparrows to wait upon him, feed him, and dance for him.

But when the night came, the darkness reminded the old man that he had a very long way to walk and need to think about taking his leave and getting back home. He thanked all of his kindly the hostess for her splendid entertainment and begged her that she would forget all about what had happened to her at the hands of his cross wife. He told Lady Sparrow that is was a great comfort and happiness to him to find that she had such an amazing home and to know that she wanted for nothing. He explained, not knowing what had happened to her and how she fared caused him anxiety. He now knew that all was well and that he could return home with a light heart. He told her that if she ever needed anything from him, she had only to send for him, and he would come at once.

The Lady Sparrow begged the old man to stay and rest with them for several days and enjoy the change of pace, but the old man explained that he had to return to his old wife, who would likely be very upset for the fact that he hadn't returned home at his regular time. He also needs to return to his wore, and as such, no matter how much he wished he could do so, he could not accept the invitation to stay. Now that he knew where his beloved Lady Sparrow lived, he could come to visit her whenever he had time.

Once Lady Sparrow saw that she would be unable to persuade the old man to stay, she gave an order to some of the servants, and they brought in two boxes. One box was large, and one was small. These were set before the old man, and the Lady Sparrow asked him to choose whichever one of the boxes he liked for a present. The old man couldn't turn this proposal and picked out the smaller of the two boxes.

He explained his choice by saying, 'I am now too old and feeble to carry the big and heavy box. As you are so kind as to say that I may take whichever I like, I will choose the small one, which will be easier for me to carry.'

All of the sparrows helped him place the box on his back, and they followed him to the gate to see him off, bidding him farewell with many bows. They asked him to come again whenever he had the time. Thus the old man left his pet sparrow quite happily. The sparrow did not show the least bit of ill-will for all of the unkindness that she had endured at the hands of his old wife. Indeed, the only thing she felt was sorrow for the old man who had to deal with it all the time.

Once the old man got back to his home, he found his wife crosser than usual, for it was very late in the night, and she had been waiting up for him to get home.

'Where have you been all this time?' she asked with anger in her voice. 'Why do you come back so late?'

The old man tried to calm his wife down by showing her the box of presents that he had returned with, and then told her everything had happened to him, and how amazing it had been to be entertained at the sparrow's house.

'Now let us see what is in the box,' the old man said, not giving her the chance to grumble once more. 'You must help me open it.' They both sat down in front of the box and opened it.

To their amazement, the box was filled to brim with silver and gold coins and many other precious items. The mats of the little cottage glittered as they removed all of the items, one by one, and placed them down and handled them again and again. The old man was over-come with joy at the sight of everything that was now his. The sparrow's gift was beyond his wildest dream. It was going to allow him to give up his work and live in ease and comfort for the rest of his life.

He said, 'Thanks to my good little sparrow! Thanks to my good little sparrow!' He repeated this phrase over and over again.

But 'Twas the old woman's evil nature, after the first few moments of satisfaction and surprise had worn off, and she could not suppress her greed. She started to blame the old man for not having brought back the large box of presents. He had innocently told her how he had refused the larger of the two boxes, preferring the smaller one as it would be lighter and easier to carry.

'You silly old man,' said the old woman, 'Why did you not bring the large box? Just think about what we have lost. We might have had twice as much silver and gold as this. You are certainly an old fool!' She screamed and huffed to bed in anger.

The old man now wished that he had never mentioned anything about the larger box, but it was too late now.

The greedy old woman, not happy with their good luck that had unexpectedly befallen them, and which she did not deserve, made up her mind to get more.

Very early the following morning, she awoke and made the old man tell her how to get to the sparrow's home. Once he realized what she was planning on doing, he tried to keep her from going, but it was of no use. She was not going to listen to a word he said. It was odd how the old woman didn't feel the least bit ashamed of going to visit the sparrow after how cruelly she had treated her. But all of that greed she had for the big box made her forget everything else. It did even dawn on her that the sparrows could be angry with her, which they were, and might punish her for what she had done.

Ever since the moment the Lady Sparrow had returned to her home in the sad state that her family had found her, bleeding and weeping from the mouth, her entire family had done little more than talk about how evil the old woman was. 'How could she?' they asked one another, 'inflict such a heavy punishment for such a trifling offense as that of eating some rice-paste by mistake? ' The loved the old man very much, who they knew was kind and good and patient under all of the troubles he had. But they despised the old woman, and they decided that if they ever had the chance, they would punish her as she deserved. They did not have long to wait.

After she walked for many hours, the old woman came upon the bamboo grove which she had demanded her husband carefully describe. She stood before it and shouted, 'Where is the tongue-cut sparrow's house? Where is the tongue-cut sparrow's house?'

At last, she noticed the eaves of the house poking out from between the bamboo foliage. She raced to the door and knocked loudly. Once, the servants told the Lady Sparrow that her old mistress was at the door, asking or her. She was quite surprised at this unexpected visit. After everything that had happened, she did not wonder a little at the boldness of the old woman in coming to her house. The Lady Sparrow, however, was polite, and so she ventured out to greet the old woman, remembering that she used to be her mistress.

The old woman did not intend to waste any time, and she got straight to the point without any shame whatsoever. She stated, 'You need not trouble to entertain me as you did, my old man. I have come myself to get the box which he so stupidly left behind. I shall soon take my leave if you give me the big box. This is all I want!'

The Lady Sparrow consented and called to her servants to bring out the big box. The old woman eagerly grabbed the box and hoisted onto her back. Without even thanking the Lady Sparrow, she started to hurry home.

The box was so hefty that she could not walk fast, much less run, as she wanted to do. She was anxious to get home and see what was inside of the box, but she found that she had to sit down and rest from time to time.

As she staggered under her heavy load, her desire to open up the box became too great to resist. She couldn't wait until she got home because she assumed that it was a box full of silver and gold, precious jewels like the small one had been.

At last, all of her greed and selfishness made her put the box down and open it carefully. She expected to gloat her eyes upon a mine of wealth. What she saw, however, so terrified her that she almost lost all of her senses. As soon as she removed the lid, several terrifying and frightful looking demons bounced out of the box and surrounded her, looking as if they intended to kill her. Never in her worst dreams had she ever seen such horrible looking creatures. A demon that had one giant eye in the middle of its forehead came forward and glared at the old woman. Monsters that had gaping mouths looked like they were going to devour her. A gigantic snake coiled and hissed around her, and a colossal frog hopped and croaked towards her.

The older woman had never felt so frightened in her life and ran away from that spot as fast as her legs could possibly carry her, glad to get away alive. Once she reaches the house, she fell to the floor and told her husband through tears about everything that had happened to her, and how she had almost been killed by the demons and monsters that had been in the box.

Then she started to blame the sparrow, but the old man quickly stopped her. He said, 'Don't blame the sparrow. It is your wickedness, which has at last met with its reward. I only hope this may be a lesson for you in the future!'

The old woman did not replay, and from that day forward, she repented of her cross, unkind behavior. She turned into a good old woman so that her husband hardly recognized her as the same person, and they spend the read of their lives happily, free from care or want, spending the treasures carefully that the old man had gotten from his pet, the tongue-cut sparrow."

CHAPTER 8

The Peach Boy – Momotaro

"A long time ago, there lived an old woman and an old man. They were peasants and worked hard to earn their rice each day. The old man would go and cut grass for the farmers around the town. While he was doing this, his wife did the housework and worked in their little rice field.

One day, the man went into the hills to cut grass, and his wife took some clothes down to the river to wash them.

It was almost summer, and the country was lovely. It was refreshing for them to see all the greenness as they went to work. The grass beside the river looked like green velvet, and the pussy willows on the edge of the water stood shaking their soft tassels.

The breeze blew and ruffled the water's surface. This turned the water into small waves. The breeze passed along and touched the cheeks of the old couple who felt very happy this particular morning. The old couple didn't know why they were so pleased, they just knew they were.

The woman finally found a spot on the river bank and placed her basket on the ground. She then began working on washing the clothes. She took each item out of the basket one by one and washed them in the river. She rubbed them on the stones to get them clean. The water was crystal clear, and she could see the small fish swimming all around. She could also see every pebble on the bottom.

While she was washing their clothes, a large peach came bumping down the stream. She looked up from washing the clothes and saw the peach. She was 60 years old, and she hadn't ever seen a peach this size in all of her life.

She thought to herself, 'How delicious that peach must be! I have to get it and take it home to my husband.'

She reached her arm out and tried to catch it, but it was out of her reach. She looked around for a stick, but there wasn't one that she could see. If she went looking for a stick, she would lose the peach.

She stopped for a moment to think about what she could do, and then she remembered an old charm. So, she started to clap her hands to keep time with the rolling peach going down the stream. While she clapped, she sang this song:

'Distant water is bitter, and the near water is sweet; pass by the distant water and come into the sweet.'

It was strange to say that as soon as she started repeating this song, the peach started getting nearer and nearer to the river bank where she was standing. It finally stopped right in front of her so that she could pick it up with her hands. She was so excited. She couldn't finish the washing because she was too excited and happy. She put all the clothes back in the basket and slung the basket onto her back. She carried the peach in her hands and hurried home.

It seemed like a very long time until her husband returned home. He was finally back home just as the sun began to set. He had a massive bundle of grass on his back. It was so large that he was almost hidden by it. She almost couldn't see him. He looked very tired and was using the scythe as a walking stick. He was leaning on it as he walked along.

When the old woman saw him, she called out to him.

'Oh, Fii San! I have been waiting for you to come home for such a long time today!'

'What is the matter? Why are you so impatient?' he asked, wondering at her eagerness that was very unusual. 'Has something happened while I was away?'

'Oh, no!' she answered. 'Nothing has happened. I just found a nice present for you!'

'That is good.' said the old man. He then washed his feet in a basin of water and stepping onto the veranda.

The woman ran into the little room and brought out the peach from the cupboard. It felt heavier than it did earlier. He held it up to him and said:

'Just look at this! Did you ever see a peach this large in your life?'

When he looked at the peach, he was astonished and said:

'This is indeed the largest peach I have ever seen! Wherever did you buy it?'

'I did not buy it.' she answered. 'I found it in the river where I was washing the clothes.'

She proceeded to tell him the story of how she was able to get the peach.

'I am thrilled that you have found it. Let us eat it now, for I am hungry.' said the old man.

He took out a kitchen knife and placed the peach on a cutting board. She was just about to cut into it when suddenly the peach split in two, and a clear voice said:

'Wait a bit, old man!' To their surprise, a beautiful child stepped out of the peach.

The old woman and her husband were astonished at what they had seen that they fell down. The child spoke one more time:

'Don't be afraid. I am no demon or fairy. I will tell you the truth. Heaven has had compassion on you. Every day and every night, you have lamented that you had no child. Your cry has been heard, and I am sent to be the son of your old age!'

Upon hearing this, the old woman and her husband were delighted. They had cried day and night with sorrow at not having a child to help them in their old age. Now their prayers had been answered; they were so full of joy that they didn't know what to do with their feet or their hands. The old man picked the child up in his arms and then passed him to the old woman. They gave him the name of Momotaro or Son of a Peach since he came out of a peach.

Years passed quickly, and the child grew strong. He was 15 years old, and he was taller and more robust than any other boy his age. He was handsome and very courageous. He was wise for his age, too. The couple's pleasure was so great when they looked at him. He was what they believed a hero should look like.

Momotaro comes to his father one day and solemnly said:

'Father, by a strange chance, we have become father and son. Your goodness to me has been higher than the mountain grasses which it was your daily work to cut, and deeper than the river where my mother washes the clothes. I do not know how to thank you enough.'

'Why,' the old man said, 'it is a matter of course that a father should bring up his some. When you are old, it will be your turn to take care of us, so after all, there will be no profit or loss between us as everyone will be equal. Indeed, I am rather surprised that you should thank me in this way!' the old man began looking bothered.

'I hope you will be patient with me,' stated Momotaro, 'but before I begin to pay back your goodness to me, I have a request to make which I hope you will grant me above everything else.'

'I will let you do whatever you wish, for you are quite different from all the other boys!'

'Then let me go away at once!'

'What do you say? Do you wish to leave your old father and mother and go away from your old home?'

'I will surely come back again if you let me go now!'

'Where are you going?'

'You must think it strange that I want to go away,' Momotaro said, 'because I have not yet told you my reason. Far away from here to the northeast of Japan, there is an island in the sea. This island is the stronghold of a band of devils. I have often heard how they invade this land, kill and rob the people, and carry off all they can find. They are not only evil, but they are disloyal to our Emperor and disobey his laws. They are also cannibals, for they kill and eat some of the poor people who are so unfortunate as to fall into their hands. These devils are very evil beings. I must go and conquer them and bring back all the plunder of which they have robbed this land. It is for this reason that I want to go away for a short time!'

The old man was very surprised when he heard this from a boy of only 15. He thought it would be best to allow the boy to go. He was fearless and strong, and other than that, the man knew the boy wasn't a common child. He had been sent to them as a gift, and he felt sure that any devil would be powerless if they tried to harm the boy.

'All that you say is very interesting, Momotaro,' the old man stated. 'I will not hinder you in your determination. You may go if you wish. Go to the island as soon as ever like and destroy the demons and bring peace to the land.'

'Thank you for all your kindness,' Momotaro stated. He began getting ready to leave that day. He was filled with courage and didn't know anything about fear.

The old woman and man began working on pounding rice on the kitchen table to make cakes for Momotaro to take with him.

The cakes were finally made, and Momotaro was ready to begin his journey.

Parting will always be sad, and it certainly was this time, too. The old people's eyes filled with tears and their voices began trembling when they said:

'Go with all speed and care. We expect you back, victorious!'

Momotaro was said to leave his parents even though he knew he would be back as quickly as possible. He knew how lonely they would be while he was gone. But he told them 'good-bye' very bravely.

'I am going now. Take care of yourselves while I am away. Good-bye!' He stepped out of their house quickly. In complete silence, Momotaro's eyes and those of his parents met in farewell.

Momotaro hurried until it was midday. He started feeling hungry, and he opened his bag and took out a race cake and sat down to eat it under a tree on the side of the road. While he was eating, he saw a dog that was almost a big as a pony came running out of the high grass. He was headed straight for Momotaro, baring his teeth, and he said fiercely:

'You are a rude man to pass my field without asking for my permission. If you leave all your cakes, you may go on your journey. If not, I will bite you until you die!'

Momotaro laughed at the dog scornfully:

'What is that you are saying? Do you know who I am? I am Momotaro, and I am on my way to subdue the devils in their island stronghold in the northeast of Japan. If you try to stop me on my way there, I will cut you in two from your head down!'

The dog's manner changed very quickly. His tail drooped between his legs, and he came near Momotaro and bowed low enough that his head touched the ground.

'What did I hear? The name of Momotaro? Are you really Momotaro? If you have often heard of your great strength. Not knowing who you were, I have behaved in a foolish way. Will you please pardon my rudeness? Are you indeed on your way to invade the Island of the Devils? If you take such a rude fellow with you as one of your followers, I shall be very grateful to you.'

'I think I can take you with me if you wish to go.' Momotaro stated.

'Thank you!' The dog said. 'By the way, I am very hungry. Will you give me one of the cakes that you are carrying?'

'This is the best kind of cake there is in Japan.' Momotaro stated. 'I cannot spare you a whole one. I will give you half of one.'

'Thank you very much.' The dog stated and took the piece that was thrown at him.

Momotaro stood up, and the dog followed him. They walked over hills and through valleys for a long time. As they walked along, an animal comes down out of a tree that was ahead of them. This creature soon walked up to Momotaro and stated:

'Good morning, Momotaro! You are welcome in this part of the country. Will you allow me to go with you?'

The dog jealously answered this creature:

'Momotaro already has a dog to accompany him. Of what use is a monkey-like you in battle? We are on our way to fight the devils! Get away from us!'

The monkey and the dog started to quarrel and bite each other because these two animals have always hated each other.

'Now, don't quarrel!' Momotaro stated. He put himself between the two. 'Wait one moment, dog!'

'It is not at all dignified for you to have such a creature as that following you!' stated the dog.

'What do you know about it?' Momotaro asked, and pushed to dog aside. He talked to the monkey:

'Who are you?'

'I am a monkey who lives in these hills.' The monkey replied. 'I heard about your expedition to the Island of the Devils, and I have come to go with you. Nothing will please me more than to follow you!'

'Do you really wish to go to the Island of the Devils and fight with me?' 'Yes, sir.' stated the monkey.

'I admire your courage,' Momotaro said. 'Here is a piece of one of my find rice cakes. Come along!'

The monkey joined Momotaro on his quest. The monkey and the dog didn't get along well and were always snapping at one another as they walked along. They always wanted to fight. This caused Momotaro too cross, and he finally sent the dog ahead with a flag and placed the monkey behind them with a sword. He put himself halfway between them with a war fan that was made from iron.

The finally came to a vast field. Here they saw a bird fly down and land on the ground right in front of their party. It was the most beautiful bird that Momotaro had ever seen. It had five different robes of feathers on his body, and its head was covered with a cap of scarlet.

The dog ran straight for the bird and grabbed it, and tried to kill it. But the bird its spurs out and flew at the dog's tail. The fight was on.

Momotaro went to the two fighting animals. He couldn't help admiring the bird. It had a lot of spirit in the fight. It would certainly make a good fighter against the devils.

He walked up to the bird and the dog and grabbed hold of the dog. He spoke to the bird:

'You rascal, you are hindering my journey. Surrender at once, and I will take you with me. If you don't, I will set this dog to bite off your head.'

The bird surrendered and begged to go with Momotaro.

'I don't know what excuse to offer for quarreling with the dog, your servant, but I did not see you. I am a miserable bird known as a pheasant. It is very generous of you to pardon my rudeness and to take me with you. Please allow me to follow behind the dog and monkey.'

'I congratulate you on surrendering so soon.' Momotaro stated, smiling. 'Come and join us in our raid on the devils.'

'Are you going to take this bird with you also?' The dog asked while interrupting.

'Why do you ask such an unnecessary question? Didn't you hear what I said? I take the bird with me because I wish to!'

The dog replied with a 'Humph!'

Momotaro stood up and gave an order:

'Now, all of you must listen to me. The first thing necessary in an army is harmony. It is a wise saying which says that advantage on earth is better than an advantage in heaven! Union amongst ourselves is better than any earthly gain. When we are not at peace amongst ourselves, it is no easy thing to subdue an enemy. From now, you three, the dog, the monkey, and the pheasant, must be friends with one mind. The one who first begins a quarrel will be discharged on the spot!'

All three animals promised not to quarrel anymore. The pheasant had become a member of Momotaro's quest and received half of a rice cake.

Momotaro's influence was so wonderful that the three became great friends and hurried on with him as their leader. Moving forward day after day, they soon came to the shore of the Northeastern Sea. There wasn't anything to be seen as far as the eye could see. There weren't any signs of any islands. The only thing breaking the stillness was the waves rolling on the shore.

Now, the pheasant, monkey, and dog had come bravely all the way through the long valley and over the hills, but they hadn't ever seen the sea. For the first time since they started on their quest, they were filled with wonder, and they looked at each other silently. How would they cross the water to get to the Island of the Devils?

Momotaro saw that they were intimidated by the sea, and he spoke roughly and loudly to them:

'Why do you hesitate? Are you afraid of the sea? Oh, what cowards you are! It is impossible to take such weak creatures as you with me to fight demons. It will be a lot better for me to go alone. I discharge you all of you right now!'

The animals were taken aback at this strong demand and clung to Momotaro's sleeve. They begged him not to send them away.

The dog pleaded, 'Please, Momotaro.'

The monkey pleaded, 'We have come thus far!'

The pheasant pleaded, 'It is inhumane to leave us here!'

'We aren't at all afraid of the sea,' stated the monkey.

The pheasant stated, 'Please take us with you!'

The dog stated, 'Do, please.'

They had all gained some courage, and Momotaro stated:

'Well, then, I will take you with me, but be careful!'

Momotaro found a small ship, and they all climbed aboard. The weather and wind were fair, and the ship went like an arrow across the sea. It was the first time any of them had been on the water, and the three animals were afraid of the rolling vessel and the waves. Little by little, they all grew more accustomed to the water and was happy once again. Each day they paced on the deck of the ship, eagerly looking for the Island of the Devils.

Once they got tired of this, they told one another stories about their exploits that they were proud of, and then they played games. Momotaro found a lot of ways to amuse himself by listening to the three animals and watching them. By doing this, he forgot that they were a long way from where they needed to be, and he was tired of this voyage and of not doing anything. He wanted to be killing monsters who had done a lot of harm to the country he loved.

While the wind blew to their favor, and they didn't meet any storms, this made their voyage very quick. One day while the sun was brightly shining, they were rewarded by the sight of land.

Momotaro knew that they had seen the Devils' stronghold. On the top of a high cliff, looking out over the sea, was a vast castle. Now that his quest was at hand, he was thinking deeply with his head in his hands. He was beginning to wonder how he should start the attack. His followers were watching him and waiting for orders. He soon called to the pheasant.

'It is a great advantage for us to have you with us,' Momotaro said to the pheasant. 'Since you have good wings, fly at once to the castle and engage the demons in a fight. We will follow you.'

The pheasant obeyed. He flew from the ship beating the air with his wings. The pheasant was soon at the island to take his position of the roof right in the center of the castle. He called out loudly:

'All you devils listen to me! The great Japanese general Momotaro has come to fight you and to take your stronghold from you. If you wish to save your lives, surrender at once, and in token of your submission, you must break off your horns that grow out of your forehead. If you don't surrender and make up your mind to fight, we, the monkey, the dog, and the pheasant, will kill you by tearing and biting you to death!'

The horned demons looked up and just saw the pheasant. They laughed at the pheasant and said:

'A wild pheasant, indeed, it is ridiculous to hear such words from a mean thing like you. Wait until you get a blow from our iron bars!'

The devils were very angry. The shook their red hair and horns fiercely and rushed to put on their tiger skin trousers. They were trying to make themselves look even more terrible. They brought out colossal iron bars and ran to where the pheasant was perched over their heads. They wanted to knock him down. The pheasant flew one way to escape the blow and then attacked the head of the demons. He flew around and around them. He beat the air with his wings ceaselessly and fiercely so that the devils started to wonder if they were fighting just one bird or many birds.

While all this was happening, Momotaro had brought the ship to land. While they were approaching the shore, he noticed that the shore was a very high cliff, and the large castle has high walls around it. The huge iron gates were fortified strongly.

Momotaro docked the boat and hoped to find some way of entering the castle. He walked up a path toward the top. He was followed by the dog and the monkey. They soon found two beautiful damsels washing their clothes in a stream. Momotaro saw that the clothes were stained with blood, and as the two maidens washed the clothes, tears were falling down their cheeks. He stopped and talked to them:

'Why are you, and why do you weep?'

'We are captives of the Demon King. We were carried away from our homes onto this island, and though we are the daughters of Daimios, we are obliged to be his servants, and one day he will kill us' at this point, the maidens held up one of the blood-stained clothes. 'He will eat us, and there isn't anyone who will help us!'

More tears burst out of them at this horrible thought.

'I will rescue you,' Momotaro stated. 'Do not weep any more; only show me how I may get into the castle.'

The maidens led the way and showed Momotaro a back door on the lowest level of the castle. The door was so small the Momotaro almost couldn't fit through.

The pheasant was still fighting hard, saw Momotaro and his band of animal rush in the back door.

Momotaro's fight was so furious that the devils couldn't stand up against him. Their foe had only been one bird at the beginning, but now Momotaro, along with the monkey and dog, had arrived, and they were confused because these four fought like a hundred. They were all so strong. Some of the devils fell off the castle's parapet and were broken to pieces on the rocks. Others fell into the sea and drowned while most were beaten to death by Momotaro and his three companions.

The chief of the devils was the only one that was left. He quickly made up his mind to surrender because he knew that his enemy was a lot stronger than a normal man.

He humbly came up to Momotaro and threw down his iron bar. He kneeled at Momotaro's feet, broke off his horns as a token os his submission because they were the sign of his power and strength.

'I am afraid of you.' the devil said meekly. 'I cannot stand against you. I will give you all the treasure hidden in this castle if you will only spare my life!'

Momotaro laughed.

'It isn't like you, devil, to beg for mercy, is it? I cannot spare your sinful life, however much you beg, for you have killed and tortured many people and robbed our country for many years.'

Then Momotaro tied the chief devil up and gave him to the monkey. After he did this, he went into all the rooms inside the castle and set all the prisoners free. He gathered all of the treasure that he could find.

The pheasant and dog carried the plunder home, and Momotaro returned to his home triumphantly. He took the chief devil as a captive. The damsels and others that the demons had carried off to be slaves were taken back to their homes safely.

The entire country made Momotaro a hero upon his return. They rejoiced that their country was now free from the devils that had been a terror of their land for a long time.

The old couple was overjoyed more than ever when Momotaro returned home with the treasure. This allowed them to live in plenty and peace until the end of their days."

CHAPTER 9

The Story of Urashima Taro, The Fisher Lad

"Many, many years ago in the province of Tango, on the shore of Japan, lived a little fishing village of Mizu-no-ye. In it lived a young fisherman named Urashima Taro. His father had been a fisherman as well, and his son had been given double the amount of skill he had. Urashima was one of the most skillful anglers in all that countryside and could catch more Tai and Bonito in a day than all of the others could in a week.

But in that little fishing village, he was known for more than being a smart fisher of the sea. He was also known for his kind heart. In his entire life, he had never hurt a soul, great or small. When he was a boy, his friends had always laughed at him because he didn't want to join in with them when they teased the animals, but he always tried to keep them from being mean to animals.

One soft summer twilight, he headed home after a long day of fishing when he reached a group of children. The group was all talking and screaming at the top of their lungs. They seemed to be very excited about something, and when he walked over to see what was going on, he saw that they were tormenting a tortoise. One of the boys pulled it this way, and then another boy pulled it that way. A third boy beat it with a stick, all while the others pulled it this way and that. Then a fourth boy hammered the shell with a stone.

Urashima felt extremely sorry for the poor tortoise and decided that he was going to rescue him. He stepped up to the boys and said, 'Look here, boys, you are treating that poor tortoise so badly that it will soon die!'

The boys, who were all at that age where children seem delighted to be cruel to animals, took no notice of Urashima's gentle reproof. Instead, they continue to tease the animal. One boy, not looking up, replied, 'Who cares whether it lives or dies? We do no. Here, boys, go on, go on!'

They started to treat the poor tortoise worse than ever before. Urashima waited a moment, thinking in his mind about what would be the best way to handle these young boys. He could try persuading them to give him the tortoise, so he smiled and said, 'I am sure you are all good, kind boys! Now, won't you give me the tortoise? I should like to have it so much!'

'No, we won't give you the tortoise,' one of the boys replied. 'Why should we? We caught it ourselves.'

'I'm sure what you are saying is true,' Urashima said, 'but I do not ask you to give it to me for nothing. I will give you some money for it. In other words, Ojisan will buy it from you. Won't that do for you, my boys?'

He held the money out to the boys, strung on a piece of string, through a hole in the center of each coin.

'Loy, boys, you can buy anything you like with this money. You can do much more with this money than you can with that poor tortoise. See what good boys you are to listen to me.'

The boys weren't naughty boys. They were simply a little mischievous, and as Urashima was talking to them, they were won over by his kind smile and gentle words. They started 'to be of his spirit,' as they say in Japan. Slowly they all came over to him. The leader of the group held out the tortoise to him.

'Very well, Ojisan, we will give you the tortoise if you will give us the money!' With that, Urashima took the tortoise and gave the boys the money. The boys called out to each other and raced away, soon out of sight of Urashima.

Once the boys were gone, Urashima started to stroke the back of the tortoise while he said, 'Oh, you poor thing! Poor thing! There, there, you're safe now. They say that a stork lives for a thousand years, but the tortoise for ten thousand years. You have the longest life of any creature in this world, and you were in great danger of having that precious life cut short by those cruel boys. Luckily I was passing by and saved you, and so life is still yours. Now I am going to take you back to your home, the sea, at once. Do not let yourself be caught again, for there might be no one to save you next time.'

During his speech to the tortoise, the kind fisherman walked quickly to the shore and out onto the rocks. Then he placed the tortoise into the water and watched the animal disappear. He then turned homewards himself, for he was tired and the sun had set.

The following morning, Urashima went out as usual in his boat. The weather was great, and the sea and sky were blue and soft in the summer morning's tender haze.

Urashima boarded his boat and dreamily pushed out to sea, throwing out a line as he did so. He was soon past the other fishing boats and left them far behind until they were lost to sight. His boat continued to drift further and further out into the blue waters. Somehow, he knew not why he felt happier than usual this morning. He couldn't help but wish that, like the tortoise he had helped the day before, he had thousands of years to live instead of the short span of human life.

He was suddenly startled out of his reverie when he heard something call his name.

'Urashima, Urashima!'

Clear as day and as soft as the summer wind, the name floated across the sea.

He stood up and gazed in the direction of the voice, thinking that one of the other boats had started to catch up to him. But try as he might, looking out over the wide expanse of water, near and far, he could not see any signs of a boat so that the voice couldn't have come from another human being.

Startled and wondering who or what had been calling to him so clearly, he looked in every direction around him and saw that a tortoise and come up to the side of his boat. Urashima was surprised to realize that it had been the very tortoise he had rescued the day before.

'Well, Mr. Tortoise,' Urashima said, 'Was it you who called my name just now?'

The tortoise quickly nodded its head several times before saying, 'Yes, it was I. Yesterday, in your good shadow, my life was saved, and I have come to offer you my thanks and to tell you how grateful I am for your kindness to me.'

'Indeed,' Urashima said, 'that is very polite of you. Come up into the boat. I would offer you a smoke, but as you are a tortoise, doubtless, you do not smoke,' and the fisherman laughed at his joke.

The tortoise joined in on the laughter as well and said, 'Sake is my favorite refreshment, but I do not care for tobacco.'

'Indeed,' Urashima said, 'I regret very much that I have no sake in my boat to offer you, but come up and dry your back in the sun. Tortoises always love to do that.'

The tortoise climbed up into the boat with the help of the fisherman, and after an exchange of some small talk, the tortoise said, 'Have you ever seen Rin Gin, the Palace of the Dragon King of the Sea, Urashima?'

The fisherman shook his head and said, 'No. Year after year, the sea has been my home, but though I have often heard of the Dragon King's realm under the sea, I have never yet set eyes on that wonderful palace. It must be very far away if it exists at all.'

'Is that really so? Have you never seen the Sea King's Palace? Then you have missed seeing one of the most wonderful sights in the whole universe. It is far away at the bottom of the sea, but if I take you there, we shall soon reach the place. If you would like to see the Sea King's land, I will be your guide.'

'I really would like to go there, certainly, and you are very kind to think of taking me, but you must remember that I am only a poor mortal and have not the power of swimming like a sea creature such as you are.'

Before the fisherman was able to say another word, the tortoise stopped, 'What? You need not swim yourself. If you ride on my back, I will take you without any trouble on your part.'

'But,' Urashima said, 'how is it possible for me to ride on your small back?'

'While it may seem odd to you, but I assure you that you can do so. Try at once! Just come and get on my back and see if it is as impossible as you think!'

Once the tortoise had finished speaking, Urashima looked at its shell. It was strange to say that he saw the creature had suddenly grown so big that a man could easily sit on it back.

'This is strong,' Urashima said, 'Mr. Tortoise, with your kind permission, I will get on your back,' he exclaimed as he jumped on.

The tortoise, unfazed by the man's weight, and as if the strange proceeding were quite ordinary, said, 'Now we will set out at our leisure.' With those words, the tortoise leaped into the sea with Urashima on his back. Down into the waters, the tortoise dove. For a long time there, two strange friends rode through the sea. Urashima never became tired, nor did his clothes every get wet from the water. At last, far in the distance, a magnificent gate appeared. Behind the gate, there stood long, sloping roofs of a palace on the horizon.

'Ah,' Urashima exclaimed, 'that looks like the gate of some large palace just appearing! Mr. Tortoise, can you tell what that palace is we can now see?'

'That is the great gate of the Rin Gin Palace. The large roof that you can see behind the gat is the Sea King's Palace itself.'

'Then we have at last come to the realm of the Sea King and to his Palace,' Urashima exclaimed.

'Yes, indeed,' answered the tortoise, 'and don't you think we have come very quickly?'

As the tortoise was speaking, the tortoise reached the side of the gate, 'And here we are, and you must please walk from here.'

The tortoise went before Urashima and spoke to the gatekeeper, saying, 'This is Urashima Taro, from the country of Japan. I have had the honor of bringing him as a visitor to this kingdom. Please show him the way.

The gatekeeper, who was a fish, quickly led him through the gate. The cuttlefish, the sole, the flounder, the red bream, and all the chief vassals for the Dragon King of the Sea now came out with courtly bows to welcome this stranger.

'Urashima Sama, Urashima Sama! Welcome to the Sea Palace, the home of the Dragon King of the Sea. Three times welcome are you, having come from such a distant country. And to you, Mr. Tortoise, we are greatly indebted to you for all your trouble in bringing Urashima here.' They turned once more to Urashima to say, 'Please follow us this way.' From that point on, the entire band of fishes became his guides.

Urashima, who was only a poor fisher lad, didn't know how to act in a palace. As strange as all this was to him, he did not feel embarrassed or ashamed. Instead, he followed his kind guides quite calmly while they led him to the inner palace.

Once he reached the entrance, a beautiful Princess with her attendant maidens came out to welcome him. She was more beautiful than any human he had ever seen. She was robed in flowing garments of soft green and red, like the underside of a wave. Gold threads shimmered through the folds of her gown. Her lovely black hair cascaded across her shoulders in the fashion of a king's daughter many hundreds of years ago. When she spoke, her voice sounds like music. Urashima found himself lost in wonder while he gazed upon her, and he could not speak. Then, it struck him that he should bow, but before he was able to make a low obeisance that Princess took him by the hand to take him into the beautiful hall, and to the seat of honor at the upper end, and asked him to sit.

Urashima Taro, it gives me great pleasure to welcome you to my father's kingdom,' the Princess said. 'Yesterday, you set free a tortoise, and I have sent for you to thank you for saving my life, for I was that tortoise. Now, if you would like, you shall live here forever in the land of eternal youth, where summer never dies and where sorrow never comes, and I will be your bride if you will, and we will live together happily forever!'

As Urashima listened to her beautiful words and gazed up her beautiful face, his heart was filled with great joy and wonder. He answered her, wondering if this was all a dream.

'Thank you a thousand times for your kind speech. There is nothing I could wish for more than to be permitted to stay here with you in this most beautiful land, of which I have often heard, but have never seen until this day. Beyond all words, this is the most wonderful place I have ever seen.'

As he spoke, a train of fishes appeared, all of them dressed in ceremonial, trailing garments. One by one, they silently entered the hall, bearing coral trays filled with delicacies of seaweed and fish. This wondrous feast was set before the bride and groom. They were celebrated with dazzling splendor, and in the realm of the Sea King, there was great rejoicing. Once the young pair pledged themselves in the wedding cup of wine, three times three, music was played, and songs were sung. The fish with golden tails and silver scales stepped in from the waves and danced for them. Urashima was enjoying himself. Never in his entire life had he enjoyed such a fantastic feast.

Once the feast came to an end, the Princess asked the groom if he wanted to walk through the palace and see all there was to behold. The happy fisherman, following his bride, was shown all of the wonders that enchanted the land where joy and youth go hand in hand. Neither time nor age could touch them. The palace had been built of coral and adorned with pearls. The beauties and wonders of the castle were so immense that they could not be put into words.

To Urashima, more wonderful than the palace was the garden that surrounded it. Here, all in one place could be seen in all four seasons. There were the beauties of summer and winter, spring and autumn, and they were all displayed in one place.

First, he looked to the east and said the cherry and plum trees in full bloom. The nightingales sang amongst the pink flowers, and butterflies flittered around. Looking to the south, he saw that all of the trees were green in the fullness of summer, and the nigh cricket and day cicada chirruped loudly. When he looked to the west, he saw the autumn maples were ablaze like a sunset sky, and the chrysanthemums were perfection. At the north, the change startled Urashima, for the ground was silver with snow, and the trees and bamboo were covered with snow. The pond was covered in a thick layer of ice.

Every day he found new joys and wonders. His happiness was so great that he forgot everything. He forgot about the home and parents he had left behind in his own country. Three days passed without his even thinking of everything that he had left behind. Then his mind came back to him, and he remembers who he really was. He remembered that he didn't belong to this beautiful land, or even to the Sea King's palace.

To himself, he said, 'Oh, dear. I must not stay here, for I have an old father and mother at home. What could have happened to them during this time? How anxious they must have been these days when I did not return as usual. I must go back at once without letting one more day pass.' He started to get ready for his journey in great haste.

He went to the Princess, his beautiful bride, and bowed low before her, and said, 'I have been delighted with you for a long time, Otohime Sama. You have been kinder to me than any words can tell, but now I must say goodbye. I must go back to my old parents.'

Otohime Sama began to weep. Sadly and softly, she replied, 'It is not well with you here, Urashima, that you wish to leave me so soon? Where is the haste? Stay with me for one more day.'

But Urashima remembered his parents, and in Japan, the duty to one's parents is stronger than anything else. It is strong even than pleasure or love, and he could not be persuaded. He replied, 'I must go. Do not think that I wish to leave you. It is not that. I must go and see my old parents. Let me go for one day, and I will come back to you.'

'That is it, then. There is nothing that I can do. I will send you back today to your father and mother. Instead of trying to convince you to stay with me for another day, I shall give you this as a token of our love. Please take this back with you.'

She brought out a beautiful lacquer box tied with a silken cord and tassels of red silk.

Urashima had been given so much from the Princess already that he felt guilt for taking another gift, and replied, 'It does not seem right for me to take yet another gift from you after all the many favors I have received at your hands, but because it is your wish I will do so. Tell me, what is this box?'

'That is the tamate-bako, and it holds something very precious. You mustn't open the box, no matter what happens. If you do open it, something dreadful will become of you. Now, promise me that you will never open this box.'

Urashima promised that he would never open the box, no matter what. After bidding goodbye to Otohime Sama, he went down to the seashore as the Princess, and her attendants followed behind him. There he found the large tortoise waiting for him.

He mounted the creature's back and was carried away over the shining sea into the East. He looked over him should wave goodbye to Otohime Sama until he could not see her anymore, and the land of the Sea King and the roofs of the palace were lost in the distance. He then turned his face eagerly towards his own land. He looked for the rising of the blue hills on the horizon in front of him.

At last, the tortoise reached the bay he knew so well, and to the shore where they had left. He walked onto the shore and looked around as the tortoise rode away back into the Sea King's realm.

There was a strange fear of the seized Urashima as he stood and looked around him. Why is his staring so fixedly on the people that walk past him, and why do they stare at him? The shore and hills are all the same, but the people that he sees walking pas are very different from those he had come to know before.

Wondering what all of this could mean, he walked quickly towards his old home. That even looked different, but a house stood on the spot, and he called out, 'Father, I have just returned.' As he was about to enter, he saw a strange man come out.

'Perhaps my parents have moved while I have been away, and have gone somewhere else,' the fisherman thought. For some reason, he started to feel strangely anxious, but he did not know why.

'Excuse me,' he said to the man who was staring at him, 'but except for the last few days, I have lived in this house. My name is Urashima Taro. Where have my parents gone while I was gone?'

A bewildered expression came over the man's face, and, still gazing intently on Urashima's face, he replied, 'What? Are you Urashima Taro?'

'Yes, I am Urashima Taro!'

The man laughed and said, 'you must not make such jokes. It is true that once upon a time, a man called Urashima Taro did live in this village, but that is a story three hundred years old. He could not possibly be alive now.'

When Urashima hear this, he became very frightened and replied, 'Please, please, you must not joke with me. I am greatly perplexed. I am really Urashima Taro, and I certainly have not lived three hundred years. Until four or five days ago, I lived on this spot. Tell me what I want to know without more joking, please.'

The men only grew more grave before he answered, 'You may or may not be Urashima Taro, I don't know, but Urashima Taro of whom I have heard is a man who lived three hundred years ago. Perhaps you are his spirit come to revisit your old home?'

'Why do you mock me?' Urashima said, 'I am no spirit! I am a living man. Do you not see my feet? And don-

don?' he stomped on the ground, first with one foot and then the other to show the man.

'But Urashima Taro lived three hundred years ago, that is all I know. It is written in the village chronicles,' the man persisted.

Urashima was overcome with bewilderment and trouble. He looked around him once more, terribly puzzled. Something in the way that everything looked was different from what he remembered before he went away. An awful feeling overcame him that what the man said may be true. It all seemed to be a strange dream. The few days he had lived in the Sea King's palace beyond the sea had not been days at all. They have been hundreds of years, and during that time, his parents had died and all of the people he had ever known. The village had written his story. It was of no use to stay here any longer. He had to return to his beautiful wife beyond the sea.

He walked back to the beach, holding the box that the Princess had given him. But which way was the right way? He would not be able to find it alone. Suddenly he remembers he had the box, the tamate-bako.

'The Princess told me when she gave me the box that I should never open it, that it held something very precious, but now that I have no home, now that I have lost everything that was dear to me here, and my heart grows thin with sadness, if I open the box, surely I will find something that is going to help me. Something that can show me how to get back to my beautiful Princess over the sea. There is nothing else that I could do. Yes, I will open the box and take a look.'

His heart consented to this act of disobedience, and he did his best to convince himself that what he was doing was the right thing. Slowly, very slowly, he untied the silk cord. Slowly, and wonderingly, he raised the lid of the box. What did he find? Strange to say that it was a purple cloud that rose out of the box in three soft wisps. In an instant, it covered his face and wavered over him as if it didn't want to go. It then floated away like vapor over the sea.

Urashima, who, up until that moment, had been a handsome and strong youth of 24, was suddenly becoming very, very old. His back doubled over with age. His hair transformed into a snowy white. His face wrinkled, and he fell down, dead, on the beach.

Poor Urashima. Because he was disobedient, he was never able to return to the Sea King's realm or to his lovely Princess beyond the sea. It is best never to be contrary to those who are wiser than for disobedience is the beginning of all the sorrows and miseries of life."

CHAPTER 10

Izanagi and Izanami – The Birth of the Gods

"A long time ago, back before the heavens and the Earth existed, everything was just a limitless, formless mass. There was no definition between in and yo, heaven and Earth, light and dark, male and female. The entire mass of existence formed an egg with the pure elements rising to the outside, forming the heavens and the impure congealing on the inside, creating the dense and dark Earth. The three divine beings called the Three Creating Deities were formed: The Deity of the August Center of the Heaven, The High August Producing Wondrous Deity, and The Divine Producing Wondrous Deity.

The massive and opaque materials from the formless mass began to gather together. In the earliest stages, for millions of years, Earth is said to have resembled oil floating upon the face of the waters. From this, a reed sprouted from the earth and grew into the heaves. This was to be called Takemah Gahanna, The High Plan of Heaven. From this reed was the eternal land ruler, Ne-no-Kuni, the first god to touch the earth. He then created the most remarkable of all the gods, a brother-sister pair, known as the divine couple. Several more were born in this way, and the last pair, the eight pairs, was Izanagi and Izanami. Their names meant 'He who invites' and 'She who invites' respectively.

The heavenly deities commanded Izanagi and Izanami to descend to the nebulous Earth to solidify Earth together. With a jeweled spear called Ama-no-Nuboko, the two traveled to the Floating Bridge of Heaven, which lay between the heaven and the Earth. What they saw below them was the world not condensed but what looked like a sea of filmy fog floating to and fro. An impure germ that would become the earth. Izanagi dipped the spear into the waters and mud.

When drawing it up, significant drops fell from the spear to the surface of Earth, creating the first island of the Japanese archipelago, the island of Onogorshima. Delighted, the two descended to the island and constructed a great pillar that reached the heavens. Izanagi and Izanami decided to get married and created a great palace called the Hall of Eight Fathoms for their wedding.

The two agreed to meet on the other side of the pillar, each walking in the other direction, the male deity to the left, and the female deity to the right. When they met each other on the other side, Izanami, the female deity, speaking first, exclaimed, 'How delightful it is to meet so handsome a youth!' To which, Izanagi, the male god, replied, 'How delightful I am to have fallen in with such a lovely maiden.' And the two consummated their relationship.

Their firstborn was a leech child. It was weak and boneless. The couple placed it on a reed boat and abandoned it in the waters. This child became known as Ebisu, the god of the fishermen. Their second was a floating island, which they also did not accept as their own. The two deities, disappointed in their failures of procreation, returned to heaven to ask the heavenly gods for the cause of their misfortunes. It turns out that the reason for their difficulties was because the woman shouldn't have spoken first when they met on the other side of the pillar.

The two returned to Earth, went around the pillar once more, and this time Izanagi, the male deity, spoke first, saying, 'How delightful to meet so beautiful a maiden.' 'How happy I am,' responded Izanami, 'that I should meet such a handsome youth.'

After their second meeting, they made many more babies. They gave birth to the eight main islands of Japan and six minor islands. They then gave birth to various deities to inhabit those islands, including the sea deity, the deity of the sea-straits, and the deities of the rivers, winds, trees, and mountains.

Last, Izanami gave birth to the first deity, which burned her genitals so badly that she died. In her agony, more gods were born from her vomit, urine, and feces. Izanagi mourned over Izanami's death, and from his tears, another deity was born. Angered, he beheaded his son, the fire deity, responsible for her death.

From the blood on his sword and the corpse of the slain son arose a number of deities as well. These included three deities of rocks, two of fire, and one of water. Longing for his deceased wife, Izanagi looked for Izanami at the land of Yomi, the underworld. In the darkness, he called for his wife to return with him to the land of the living. She replied that it was too late, and she had already consumed the food in the land of Yomi.

However, she would ask the gods of the underworld for permission to leave. She asked Izanagi to do one thing: to not look at her as she did this. After she left, Izanagi eventually grew impatient and decided to go look for her. He broke off the end of a comb in his hair and set it on fire to use as a light.

When he found her, he was shocked to find his once beautiful wife to be a rotting corpse being consumed by maggots. In this state, she was giving birth to the eight gods of thunder. Repulsed by this sight, Izanagi drew back and cried out.

Ashamed and angered to be seen in this condition, she chased Izanagi out of the underworld, sending the eight deities of thunder, which were born from her body, after him, and then pursued him herself.

As he reached for a huge rock to close the passage to the underworld, she shouted in anger, 'If you behave in this way, I will strangle and kill one thousand men of your land every day!'

Izanagi replied, 'If you do this, I will, every day, give life to 1500. So in one day, indeed, 1000 men will die, and, indeed, 1500 are going to be born.'

Izanagi returned home, leaving Izanami to rule the underworld; feeling unclean from his contact with the dead, he bathed himself to remove himself of all the uncleanliness through a purification ceremony by the river. As he stripped his clothing, 12 deities were born from the robes and accessories. More gods arose as he cleansed himself of the impurities of Yomi, shaking off the curse, and washing his body.

In the last step of the purification ceremony, Izanagi washed his left eye, from which Amaterasu was born.

From his right eye, Tsukuyomi was born. From his nose, Takehayasusanoo was taken. The three gods are called the 'Three precious children,' gods of the sun, the moon, and the seas. Proud of these creations, Izanagi divided his kingdom among them.

It was Amaterasu, whose name means 'shining in heaven,' who sent Japan's first ruler from the heavens to Japan, so the Emperors of Japan are considered divine and direct descendants of Amaterasu."

CHAPTER 11

Tsukuyomi and the Creation of Day and Night

" At the beginning of time, Izanagi-no-Mikoto and Izanami-no-Mikoto produced three children, Amaterasu, Tsukiyomi, and Susanoo. Amaterasu means *shining in heaven,* and she would go on to become a principal deity for the Shinto religion. Tsukuyomi, who was her brother and husband, was the god of the moon.

At the beginning of their existence, Amaterasu and her brother Tsukuyomi took care of the skies together. She would rule the day as the sun, and he would rule the night as the moon. Their brother, Susanoo, the god of storms and ruler of the seas, was cast from the heavens because of his bad behavior. But the harmony between the two would not last forever.

One day Ukemochi, the goddess of food, threw a grand feast. Amaterasu was unable to make it to the feast, so she sends her brother in her place. However, the feast took a turn for the worse and did not turn out as Uke-mochi had planned. It was discovered that Ukemochi had prepared the feast using her own bodily fluid.

She made the following meals as follows. Ukemochi faced the ocean and spat out fish. She faced the forest and, from her mouth, emerged wild game. Then she faced the rice fields and coughed up a bowl of rice. It is also said that she created other food from other parts of her body as well.

The meal, and the way in which it had been prepared, did not sit well with Tsukuyomi. Angered by his over-whelming disgust, Tsukuyomi brutally killed Ukemo-chi at her own feast. Her dead body sprang up grains, such as rice, millet, and wheat. From her eyebrows came silkworms.

Once news of what had transpired at the feast reached Amaterasu, she could not be consoled. Amaterasu pronounced her brother, Tsukuyomi, as an evil god, Amaterasu declared that she would never see her brother again. From that point on, day and night would forever remain separate."

CHAPTER 12

The Journey of Yomi

"A darkened chamber, labored breathing, a scream, a cry, blazing light, and then silence. Things should have been grand and amazing. It should have been a great day. An exalted day. A new child was to be welcomed into the family of the gods. The youngest of the deities, Izanagi and Izanami, were to have another child, but this child would be Kagutsuchi, the incarnation of fire. As one could imagine, his birth was not an easy one. He burned his mother, Izanami, and from that she died.

Enraged, Izanagi drew his sword and sliced the child into eight pieces. Those eight pieces would become the eight great volcanoes of Japan. The blood that dripped off the tip of Izanagi's sword became gods in their own right, and, thus, the god of the sea and the god of the rain came into being.

Before this terrible fate befell Izanami, death was unknown to the world, but now it had become a reality.

Izanagi was not willing to accept the faith of his be-loved wife. He decided that he was going to find her, so he descended into the realm of the dead.

As he traversed into this unknown land, he found that everything was shadowed; dim-lit, and insubstantial. It was very much a dark reflection of the world above. Stumbling about in the darkness, he searched and searched for his wife. Until, finally, he found Izanami! The problem was, he was unable to make out her face as she was hidden in the shadows. Little did he know, she had a good reason for this.

He was certain that it was Izanami, though, so he asked her to join him once again in the realm of the brightness and light. 'I cannot,' she replied, 'I have already consumed the food that has been prepared on the Heart of the Land of the Dead.'

Izanagi was not one to take no for an answer and insisted that she come back with him. He was not going to return back to Earth without her by his side. Finally, Izanami agreed, but she said she would need a bit of time to rest and to check with the rulers of Yomi to get their permission for her to leave. Before everything was said and done, Izanami made Izanagi agree to one condition.

'As I sleep and rest, you are not to look upon me,' Izanami stated.

Izanagi agreed to the condition, and Izanami retired to her chamber to sleep. Time passed, and Izanagi began to worry and grow impatient. As more time passed, he became overwhelmed with curiosity and concern. He entered the room where Izanami slept. In the darkness of the room, he could not see anything, so he broke a piece off of the comb he wore in his hair and lit it to use as a light.

Izanami was not the same person that Izanagi remembered. She had become meat that was rotting and hanging off of her bones. She was a decomposing body that was swarmed by insects and maggots. He could see her skull through her skin.

In the horror of what he was seeing, Izanagi ran out of the room, but the light and sound woke Izanami, and she began to wail and shriek. She let out a piercing cry and began to chase her faithless companion who had only loved her while she had the grace and beauty of the lighted world.

Izanami called on the Shikome, the demon women of the underworld, to seize Izanagi. The demon women chased Izanagi, but Izanagi did what any right-minded person clearly in possession of his wits would do. He took off his headdress and tossed it at the demon. As he does so, it transformed into a bunch of grapes. The grapes hit the monster, and she stops to eat them. This did not slow the demons down much, and the Shikome hot on the heels of Izanagi once more.

This time, he uses his comb. Pulling out some of the teeth, he threw them at the Shikome. The teeth of the comb become bamboo shoots and stick into the Shikome. Shikome is still right behind Izanagi. Up ahead, Izanagi sees a tree and does the only reasonable thing and God could do. He creates a river at the tree using his own urine. This slows down the Shikome, but it doesn't stop her pursuit of Izanagi.

So, Izanagi pulls out some peaches. He tosses the peaches towards the Shikome, and something about the peaches stops the Shikome. They allow him to reach the entrance of the Underworld. He strains all of his godly might and pushes a giant boulder in front of the mouth of the Land of the Dead. But just as the boulder is sealing the dark lands for good, he hears the voice of

Izanami shriek. She screams that because he deserted her just because she no longer looked as she did in the land of the living, she will kill a thousand people every day.

Izanagi, being the mature god that he is, responds by saying, 'If you do that, I will give life to 1500 every day.'

And thus, with that last statement, he leaves the underworld behind to purify himself. As the water pours down from his body, gods spring from the drops. With Amaterasu, the goddess of the sun, coming from the waters streaming from his right eye, and Tsukuyomi, the god of the moon, coming from his left. Lastly, Susanoo, the god of the storms, comes from the water dripping off of his nose.

After his purification is completed, Izanagi splits the living world between them.

Amaterasu is sent to rule over the day. Tsukuyomi is sent to rule over the night.

Susanoo is sent to rule over the rolling seas."

CHAPTER 13

The Happy Hunter and The Skillful Fisher

"Many years ago, Japan was ruled by Hohodemi, the fourth Mikoto in descent from the illustrious Amaterasu, the Sun Goddess. Not only was he handsome like his ancestress was beautiful, but he was very brave and strong. He was also famous for being the greatest hunter in the land. Because his skill was unmatched, he was called Yama-Sachi-Hiko or The Happy Hunter of the Mountains.

He had an older brother who was a skillful fisher, and since he outmatched all of his rivals in fishing, he was known as Unii-Sachi-Hiko or the Skillful Fisher of the Sea. The brothers led happy lives, thoroughly enjoying their own occupations, and the days passed happily and quickly while they each pursued their own way, the one hunting, and the other fishing.

One day came about, and the Happy Hunter went to his brother, the Skillful Fisher, and said, 'Well, my brother, I see you go to the sea every day with your fishing rod in your hand, and when you return, you come laden with fish. And as for me, it is my pleasure to take my bow and arrow and to hunt the wild animals up the mouths and down in the valleys. For a long time, we have each followed our favorite occupation, so that now we must both be tired, you of your fishing and I of my hunting. Would it not be wise for us to make a change? Will you try hunting in the mountains, and I will go and fish in the sea?'

The skillful fished quietly listened to his brother, and for a moment, thinking about what he had said, but at last, he answered, 'Oh yes, why not? Your idea is not at bad one at all. Give me your bow and arrow, and I will set out at once for the mounts and hunt for game.'

Things were settled then, and the two brothers each started out to try the occupation of the other, little thinking about what could happen. It was very unwise of them, for the Happy Hunter knew nothing of fishing, and the Skillful Fisher, who had a bad temper, knew as much about hunting.

The Happy Hunter grabbed up his brother's much-prized fishing hook and rod and went down to the seashore and sat down on the rocks. He baited the hook and cast out into the sea clumsily. He sat and gazed at the little float bobbing up and down in the water, and longed for a good fish to come and be caught. Every time the buoy moved a little, he would pull on the rob, but there was never a fish at the end of it, only the hook and bait. If he had known how to fish correctly, he would have been able to catch plenty of fish, but he was the most excellent hunter and could not help being the most bungling fisher.

The entire day passed in this way. All he did was sit on the rocks holding the fishing rod and waiting in vain for his luck to turn. At last, the day grew darker, and the evening came. Still, he had caught not a single fish. Reeling his line back in for the last time before heading home, he found that he had lost his hook without even knowing when he had dropped it.

He was now distraught, for he knew that his brother would be angry at the fact that he had lost his hook because it was his only one. He valued that hook above all other things. The Happy Hunter is now set to work to look among the rocks and the sand for the lost hook, and while he searches to and fro, his brother arrived. He had not managed to hunt any game during the day and was not only in a bad mood, but looked fearfully cross. When he noticed the Happy Hunter searching around on the shore, he knew that something must have gone wrong, so he said,

'What are you doing, my brother?'

The Happy Hunter went forward hesitantly, for he was afraid of his brother's anger, and replied, 'Oh, my brother, I have indeed done badly.'

'What is the matter? What have you done?' asked the elder brother impatiently.

'I have lost your precious fishing hook.'

As he spoke, his brother stopped him and cried out fiercely.

'Lost my hook! It is just what I expected. For this reason, when you first proposed your plan of switching our occupations, I was really against it, but you seemed to wish it so much that I gave in and allowed you to do as you wish. The mistake of our trying unfamiliar tasks is soon seen! And you have done badly. I will not return you your bow and arrow until you have found my hook. Look to it that you find it and return it to me quickly.'

The Happy Hunter felt that he was to blame for all that had happened and took his brother's scornful scolding with patience and humility. He hunted everywhere for the hook, but he could not find it anywhere. He finally had to give up all hope of finding it. He then went home, and in desperation, broke his beloved sword into pieces and made five hundred hooks out of it.

He took these to his angry brother and offered them to him, asking for his forgiveness, and begging him to accept them in the place of the one had lost for him. It was useless, though. His brother wasn't even willing to listen to him, much less grant his request.

The Happy Hunter made an additional five hundred hooks and took them to his brother, begging him once more to forgive him.

'Though you make a million hooks,' said the Skillful Fisher, shaking his head, 'they are of no use to me. I cannot forgive you unless you bring me back my own hook.'

Nothing was going to make the Skillful Fisher happy because he had always disliked his brother because of his virtues, and now with the excuse of the lost fishing hook, he planned to kill him and to take over as ruler of Japan. The Happy Hunter knew all this full well, but he could say nothing because he was the younger brother, he owed his elder obedience. He returned once more to the seashore and began to look for the missing hook. He was depressed by this because he had lost all hope of ever finding his brother's hook. As he stood on the beach, filled with wonder and perplexed over what he should do next, and old man suddenly appeared, carrying a stick in his hand. The Happy Hunter realized that he had not seen from where the old man had appeared; neither could he remember how he was there. He had simply looked up and sawed the old man coming towards him.

'You are Hohodemi, the Augustness, sometimes called the Happy Hunter, are you not?' asked the old man, 'What are you doing alone in such a place?'

'Yes, I am he,' answered the unhappy young man. 'Unfortunately, while fishing, I lost my brother's precious fishing hook. I have hunted this shore all over, but I cannot find it, and I am distraught. My brother will not forgive me until I give it back to him, but who are you?'

'My name is Shiwozuchino Okina, and I live nearby on this shore. I am sorry to hear what misfortune has befallen you. You must, indeed, be anxious. But if I tell you what I think, the hook is nowhere here. It is either at the bottom of the sea or in the body of some fish who has swallowed it and for this reason, even if you spent your entire life searching for it here, you will never find it.'

'Then what can I do?' asked the distressed man.

'You had better go down to Ryn Gu and tell Ryn Jin, the Dragon King of the Sea, what your trouble is and ask him to find the hook for you. I think that would be the best way.'

'Your idea is a splendid one,' said the Happy Hunter, 'but I fear I cannot get to the Sea King's realm, for I have always heard that it is situated at the bottom of the sea.'

'Oh, there will be no difficulty about your getting there,' said the old man, 'I can soon make something for you to ride on through the sea.'

'Thank you,' said the Happy Hunter, 'I shall be very grateful to you if you will be so kind.'

The old man set to work at once, and soon had a basket made and offered it to the Happy Hunter. He took the basked with joy, and taking it over to the water, he mounted it and prepared to set out. He bade goodbye to the kind old man who had helped him with so much and told him that he would reward him as soon as he found his hook and made his return to Japan without fear of his angry brother. The old man pointed him in the direction he needed to take, and told him how to reach the realm of Ryn Gu, and watch as he rode out to sea on the basket, which looked a lot like a small boat.

That Happy Hunter traveled as quickly as possible, riding on the basket which had been given to him by a friend. His odd little boat seemed to go through the water on its own, and the distance was much shorter than he had expected because, in a few hours, he caught sight of the gate and roof of the Sea King's Palace. It was quite a large place, with a numberless amount of sloping roofs and gables, its giant gateways, and its gray stone walls. He quickly landed and left his basket on the beach; he walked to the large gateway. The pillars of the gate had been made of beautiful red coral, and the entrance itself was decorated with glittering gems of all kinds. Large katsura trees overshadowed it. The Happy Hunter had often heard of the wonders of the Sea King's Palace beneath the sea, but all the stories he had ever heard fell short of the reality which he now saw for the first time.

The Happy Hunter wanted to walk through the gate right then and there, but he saw that it was closed, and also saw that there was no one around who could open it for him. He stopped a moment to think about what he should do. As he stood in the shade of the trees in front of the gate, he noticed a well full of fresh spring water. Surely someone would come out to draw water from the well, he thought. He climbed up into the tree that overhung the well, and seated himself to rest on one of the branches, and waited for what he hoped would happen. It wasn't long before he saw the huge gate swing open, and two beautiful women came out. Now the Mikoto had always heard that Ryn Gu was the realm of the Dragon King under the Sea and had naturally assumed that the place was inhabited by dragons and other similar creatures, so that when he saw these two lovely princesses, whose beauty was rare even in the world from where he had just come, he was extremely surprised, and wondered what it could mean.

He didn't say anything. Instead, he silently gazed at them through the leaves of the trees, waiting to see what they would do. He saw that they were carrying golden

buckets. Slowly and gracefully in their lovely garments, they walked up to the well, standing in the shade
of the katsura trees, and were about to gather water and
still unaware of the stranger watching over the. The
Happy Hunter was very well hidden in the branches of
the tree where he had taken post.

As the women leaned over the side of the well to drop
their golden buckets in, which they did every day, they
saw a reflection in the deep still water of the face of a
handsome man gazing at them from amidst the
branches of the trees. They had never seen the face of
a mortal man before. They were frightened and drew
back quickly, still holding their golden buckets. Their
curiosity, however, got the better of them, and they
glanced carefully up to see if they could spot what created the reflection. That's when they noticed the Happy
Hunter sitting in the tree looking down at them with
admiration and surprise. They gazed at him face to face,
but their tongues were still filled with surprise and
could not find a word to say to him.

Once the Mikoto noticed that he had been discovered,
he jumped carefully out of the tree and said, 'I am a
traveler, and as I was very thirsty, I came to the well in
the hopes of quenching my thirst, but I could find no
bucket with which to draw the water. So I climbed into

the tree to wait for someone to come. Just at that moment, while I was thirstily and impatiently waiting, you noble ladies appeared, as if in answer to my great need. Therefore, I pray you of your mercy, give me some water to drink, for I am a thirsty traveler in a strange land.'

His manners and graciousness rid the ladies of their timidity, and as they bowed in silence, they both walked back over to the well and dropped the golden buckets down and drew up some water. They poured it into a jeweled cup and offered it up to the stranger.

He took the cup in both hands, and raised it to the height of his forehead in token of high respect and pleasure, and then quickly drank the water, for his thirst was great. Once he had finished all of the water, he sat the cup down on the edge of the well, and drew out his short sword and cut off one of the strange curved jewels from the necklace that he wore around his neck. He dropped the gem into the cup and handed it back to the ladies.

Bowing deeply, he said, 'This is a token of my thanks.'

That ladies took the cup from him, and looking into it to see what he had put inside, for they were not sure of what it was, they gave a start of surprise. At the bottom of the cup laid a beautiful gem.

'No ordinary mortal would give away a jewel so freely. Will you honor us by telling us who you are?' said the older lady.

'Certainly,' said the Happy Hunter, 'I am Hohodemi, the fourth Mikoto, also called in Japan, the Happy Hunter.'

'Are you indeed Hohodemi, the grandson of Amaterasu, the Sun Goddess?' asked the lady who had spoken first, 'I am the eldest daughter of Ryn Jin, the King of the Sea, and my name is Princess Tayotama.'

'And,' said the younger maiden, who at last found her tongue, 'I am her sister, the Princess Tamayori.'

'Are you indeed the daughters of Ryn Jin, the King of the Sea? I cannot tell you how glad I am to meet you,' said the Happy Hunter. Without waiting for them to reply, he continued by saying, 'The other day I went fishing with my brother's hook and dropped it, how, I am sure I cannot say. As my brother prizes his fishing hook above all his other possessions, this is the greatest calamity that could have befallen me. Unless I find it again, I can never hope to win my brother's forgiveness, for he is furious at what I have done. I have searched for it many many times, but I cannot find it. Therefore I am much troubled. While I was hunting for the hook, in great distress, I met a wise old man, and he told me that the best thing I could do was to come to Ryn Gu, and to Ryn Jin, the Dragon

Kind of the Sea, and ask him to help me. This kind, old man also showed me how to come. Now you know how I got here and why. I want to ask Ryn Jin if he knows where the lost hook is. Will you be so kind as to take me to your father? And do you think he will see me?' asked the Happy Hunter.

Princess Tayotama listened to this long story and then said, 'Not only is it easy for you to see my father, but he will be much pleased to meet you. I am sure he will say that good fortune has befallen him, that so great and noble a man as you, the grandson of Amaterasu, should come down to the bottom of the sea.'

She turned to her younger sister and said, 'Do you not think so, Tamayori?'

'Yes, indeed,' answered the Princess Tamayori, in her sweet voice. 'As you say, we can know no greater honor than to welcome the Mikoto to our home.'

'Then, I ask you to be so kind as to lead the way,' said the Happy Hunter.

'Please, enter, Mikoto,' said both of the sisters, and bowing low, they led him through the gate.

The younger princess left her sister to take charge of the Happy Hunter. She walked faster than them and reached the Palace first. She sprinted to her father's room and told him of all that had happened to them at the gate, and that her sister was bringing in the Mikoto. The Dragon King of the Sea was very surprised by this news because it was seldom, perhaps once every hundred years, that the Sea King's Palace was visited by mortals.

Ryn Jin clapped his hands and summoned all of his courtiers and the servants of the Palace, and the chief fish of the sea together, and solemnly told them that the grandson of the Sun Goddess, Amaterasu, was coming to visit the Palace. He said that they must be very ceremonious and polite in serving the visitor. He orders them all to the entrance of the Palace to welcome the Happy Hunter.

Ryn Jin put on his ceremonial robes and went out to welcome him. After a few moments, the Princess Tayotama and the Happy Hunter reached the entrance, and the Sea King and his wife bowed to the ground and thanked him for the honor he did them in coming to see them. The Sea King then led the Happy Hunter to a guest room, and after he took a seat, the Sea King respectfully bowed before him and said, 'I am Ryn Jin, the Dragon King of the Sea, and this is my wife. Please, remember us forever.'

'Are you truly Ryn Jin, the King of the Sea, of whom I have so often heard?' asked the Happy Hunter, saluting his host. 'I must apologize for all the trouble I am giving you by my unexpected visit.' He bowed again and thanked the Sea King.

'You need not thank me,' said Ryn Jun. 'It is I who must thank you for coming. Although the Sea Palace is a poor place, as you see, I shall be highly honored if you will make us a long visit.'

The Sea King and the Happy Hunter were pleased, and they sat and talked for some time. At last, the Sea King clapped his hands, and then a huge school of fish appeared, all dressed in ceremonial robes and carrying various trays of sea delicacies. A great feast was spread before the King and his guest. All the fishes-in-waiting were chosen from amongst the finest fish in the sea, so one can imagine what a wonderful array of sea creatures it was that waited upon the Happy Hunter that day. Everybody in the Palace did their best to please him and to show him that he was a much-honored guest. During the last course, which lasted for hours, Ryn Jin commanded his daughters to play some music, and then the two Princesses came forward and performed on the KOTO, and sand and danced in turns. The time passed with such ease that the Happy Hunter forgot all about his trouble and why he had visited the Sea King's Realm. He allowed himself to get caught up in the enjoyment of this wonderful place. But it wasn't long before the Mikoto remembered why he had come to Ryn Gu and said to his host,

'Perhaps your daughters have told you, King Ryn Jin, that I have come here to try and recover my brother's fishing hook, which I lost while fishing the other day. May I ask you to be so kind as to inquire of all your subjects if any of them have seen a fishing hook lost in the sea?'

'Certainly,' said the Sea King, 'I will immediately summon them all here and ask them.'

As soon as he had issued the command, the plaice, the shrimp, the jellyfish, the eel, the oxtail fish, the bonito, the cuttlefish, the octopus, and many other fish of all kinds came in and sat down before the King. They made sure to arrange themselves and their fins in order. The Sea King then said,

'Our visitor who is sitting before you all is the august grandson of Amaterasu. His name is Hohodemi, the fourth Augustness, and he is also called the Happy Hunter of the Mountains. While he was fishing the other day upon the shore of Japan, someone robbed him of his brother's fishing hook. He had come all this way down to the bottom of the sea to our Kingdome because he thought that one of your fishes might have taken the hook from him in mischievous play. If any of you have done so, you must immediately return it, or if any of you know who the thief is, you must at once tell us his name and where he is now.'

All of the fishes were taken aback at these words and could say nothing for some time. They sat and looked at each other and at the Dragon King. At last, the cuttlefish came forward and said, 'I think the red bream must be the thief who has stolen the hook.'

'Where is your proof?' asked the King.

'Since yesterday evening, the red bream has not been able to eat anything, and he seems to be suffering from a bad throat. For this reason, I think the hook may be in his throat. You had better send for him at once.'

All of the fish agreed to this and said, 'It is certainly strange that the red bream is the only fish who has not obeyed your summons. Will you send for him and inquire into the matter. Then our innocence will be proved.'

'Yes,' said the Sea King, 'it is strange that the red bream has not come, for he ought to be the first to be here. Send for him at once!'

Without waiting for the King's order, the cuttlefish had already started for the red bream's dwelling. He quickly returned, bringing the red bream with him. He led him before the King. The red bream sat there looking frightened and a bit ill. He was certainly in pain, for his usually red face was pale, and his eye was nearly closed and looked but half their usual size.

'Answer, oh red bream,' cried the Sea King, 'why did you not come in answer to my summons today?'

'I have been ill since yesterday,' he answered, 'that is why I could not come.'

'Don't say another word,' cried Ryn Jin angrily, 'Your illness is the punishment of the gods for stealing the Mikoto's hook.'

'It is only too true,' said the red bream, 'the hook is still in my throat, and all my efforts to get it out have been useless. I can't eat, and I can scarcely breathe, and each moment I feel that it will choke me, and sometimes it gives me great pain. I had no intention of stealing the Mikoto's hook. I heedlessly snapped at the bait, which I saw in the water, and the hook came off and stuck in my throat. So I hope you will pardon me.'

The cuttlefish now came forward and said to the King, 'What I said was right. You see, the hook still sticks in the red bream's throat. I hope to be able to pull it out in the presence of the Mikoto, and then we can return it to him safely.'

'Please pull it out quickly,' cried the red bream, pitifully, for he felt the pains in his throat coming on once more, 'I do so want to return the hook to Mikoto.'

'Alright,' said the cuttlefish's friend, and as he opened the red bream's mouth as wide as he could, he placed one of his feelers down the throat of the red bream and quickly and easily drew the hook out of the fishes mouth. He washed it and then brought it to the King.

Ryn Jin took the hook from his subject, and then respectfully returned it to the Happy Hunter, who was overjoyed at getting the hook back. He thanked Ryn Jin many times, his face beaming with gratitude, and said that he owed the happy ending of his quest to the Sea King's wise authority and kindness.

Ryn Jin now wanted to punish the red bream, but the Happy Hunter begged him not to do so because his lost hook had been recovered but didn't want to make any more trouble for the poor red bream. The red bream had taken the hook, but he had already suffered plenty for his fault if fault it could be called. What had been done was done in heedlessness and not my intention. The Happy Hunter said he blamed himself. If he had understood how to fish properly, he would never have lost the hook in the first place. Therefore, all this trouble had been caused in the first place by his trying to do something which he did not know how to do. He begged the Sea King to forgive his subject.

Who could resist the pleading of such a wise and compassionate person? Ryn Jin forgave his subject at once at the request of the Mikoto. The red bream was so glad that he shook his fins for joy, and he and all of the other fish left, praising the virtues of the Happy Hunter.

Now that he had the hook, the Happy Hunter had nothing to keep him in Ryn Gu, and he was anxious to return to his one home and make peace with his angry brother. However, the Sea King, who had come to love him and would gladly like to keep him as a son, begged him not to go so soon, but to make the Sea Palace his home as long as he wanted. While the Happy Hunter was thinking, the Princesses, Tayotama, and Tamayori came and joined their father in begging him to stay. If he turned them down, he would seem ungracious and was obliged to stay with them for some time.

The Happy Hunter found that three years had passed by quickly in this pleasant land. The years will pass by quickly when anybody is truly happy, but while the wonders of the enchanted land seemed to be new every day, and while the Sea King's kindness seemed to grow with each passing day, the Happy Hunter grew more homesick. He could no longer repress his anxiety to know what had happened to his home, his country, and his brother while he had been away.

At last, he went to the Sea King and said, 'My stay with you here has been most happy, and I am very grateful to you for all of your kindness, but I govern Japan, and, delightful as this place is, I cannot absent myself forever from my country. I must also return the fishing hook to my brother and ask his forgiveness for having deprived him of it for so long. I am indeed very sorry to part from you, but this time it cannot be helped. With your gracious permission, I will take my leave today. I hope to make you another visit someday. Please give up the idea that I will stay any longer.'

King Ryn Jin was filled with sorrow at the thought that he had to lose his friend who had made a great diversion in the Palace of the Sea, and his tears fell fast as he replied,

'We are indeed very sorry to part you, Mikoto, for we have enjoyed your stay with us very much. You have been a noble and honored guest, and we have heartily made you welcome. I quite understand that as you govern Japan, you ought to be there and not here and that it is vain for us to try and keep you longer with us, even though we would love to have you stay. I hope you will not forget us. Strange circumstances have brought us together, and I trust the friendship thus begun between the Land, and the Sea will last and grow strong than it has ever been before.'

After the Sea King had finished his speech, he turned to his daughters and asked them to bring him the two Tide-Jewels of the Sea. The princesses bowed low, rose, and glided out of the hall. After a few minutes, they came back, and each was carrying a flashing gem which filled the room with light. As the Happy Hunter looked at them, he wonders what they could be. The Sea King took them and said to his guest,

'These two valuable talismans we have inherited from our ancestors from time immemorial. We now give them to you as a parting gift in token of our great affection for you. These two gems are called the nanjiu and the kanjiu.'

The Happy Hunter bowed low and said, 'I can never thank you enough for all of your kindness to me. And now will you add one more favor to the rest and tell me what these jewels are and what I am to do with them?'

'The naniju,' replied the Sea King, 'is also called the Jewel of the Flood Tide, and whoever hold it in his possession can command the sea to a roll in and to flood the land at any time that he wills. The kaniju is also called the Jewel of the Ebbing Tide, and this gem controls the sea and the waves thereof, and will cause even a tidal wave to recede.'

Ryn Jin then showed his friend how to use the talismans one by one and handed them to him. The Happy Hunter was very glad to have been given these wonderful gems to take back with him. He felt as though they would preserve him in case of danger from enemies at any time. After thanking his kind host, again and again, he prepared for his departure. The Sea King and the princesses, and all of the people of the Palace came out to say goodbye. Before the sound of the last farewell had died away, the Happy Hunter passed out from under the gateway, past the well of a happy memory that stood in the shade of the Katsura trees on his way to the beach.

It was here that he found, instead of the odd basket he had used to reach the Realm of Ryn Gu, an enormous crocodile waited for him. Never had he witnessed such a fantastic creature. It measured eight fathoms in length from the top of his nose to the top of its tail. The Sea King had ordered the monster to carry the Happy Hunter back to Japan. Just like the basked that Shiwozuchino Okina had made, it could travel faster than any steamboat, and riding on the back of a crocodile, the Happy Hunter returned to his homeland.

Once the crocodile made landfall, the Happy Hunter raced to tell the Skillful Fisher of his safe return. He then returned the fishing hook to his brother, which has been the cause of so much trouble between the two of them. He earnestly begged his brother to forgive him, telling him all that had happened to him in the Sea King's Palace and what an amazing adventure had led to the finding of the hook.

The Skillful Fisher had long used this lost hook as his excuse for driving his brother out of the country. When his brother had left that day three years ago and did not return, he had been delighted in his evil heart and had taken over his brother's place as ruler of the land, and had become quite rich and powerful. Now while enjoying what did not belong to him and hoped that his brother would never return to claim what was rightfully his. As one would suspect, it was quite unexpected that there stood the Happy Hunter before him.

The Skillful Fisher feigned forgiveness, for he could not make any more excuses for sending his brother away, but in his heart, he was still very angry and hated his brother more than ever. He was no longer able to bear the sight of him day after day and planned and watched for the right chance to kill him.

One day, the Happy Hunter was walking through the rice fields, and his brother followed close behind him with a dagger. The Happy Hunter knew that his brother was behind him and wanted to kill him. He felt as though, now, in this hour of great danger, was the time to use the Jewels of the Flow and Ebb of the Tide and prove if what the Sea King had told was true or not.

He took out the Jewel of the Flood Tide from his dress and raised it to his forehead. Instantly, over the fields and farms of the sea came rolling in waves until it reached the spot where his brother stood. The Skillful Fish stood, amazed and terrified, to see what was happening. In just a minute, he was struggling in the water and calling out to his brother to help save him from drowning.

The Happy Hunter had a kind heart and could not watch his brother in distress. He quickly put the Jewel of the Flood Tide back and brought out the Jewel of the Ebb Tide. No sooner had he held it up to his forehead than the sea ran back and back, and soon the rolling floods had vanished, and everything appeared as it had before.

The Skillful Fisher was very frightened by his near-death experience and was greatly impressed by the wonderful things he had seen his brother do. He realized that he was making a fatal mistake to set himself against his brother. He saw now that his brother as so powerful that he could command the sea to flow in and out. He humbled himself before the Happy Hunter and asked him to forgive him for all of the wrongs he had done him. The Skillful Fisher promised to restore his brother to his rights and swore that while the happy hunter may be the younger brother and owed him allegiance by right of birth, that he, the Skillful Fisher, would exalt him as his superior and bow to him as the Lord of all Japan.

Then the Happy Hunter said that he would forgive his brother if he would throw into the receding tide all his evil ways. The Skillful Fisher promised, and there was peace between the two of them. From this time on, he kept his word and became a good man and a kind brother.

The Happy Hunter ruled his land once more without being disturbed by family strife, and there was peace in Japan for a very long time. Above all the treasures in his house, he prized the two jewels that had been given to him by Ryn Jin, the Dragon King of the Sea."

CHAPTER 14

The Strong Boy – Kintaro

"A long time ago, there lived a brave soldier Kintoki. He lived in Kyoto. He fell in love with a beautiful woman and married her. It wasn't long after this, due to some trouble that his friends caused, his reputation declined with the Courts, and they dismissed him. This misfortune upset him so much that he died soon after. He left behind his young wife to face the world by herself.

She was afraid of her husband's enemies, and she went into the Ashigara Mountains right after her husband died. It was there in the forests where nobody ever went that she gave birth to a boy. She named him Kintaro or the Golden Boy. The wonderful thing about this little boy was his amazing strength. He only got stronger as he grew up. By the time he was eight, he could cut down trees as fast as any of the woodcutters. His mother gave him a large ax, and he would go into the forest to help the woodcutters chop down trees. He soon got the nickname of *Wonder Child.* The woodcutters gave his mother a nickname of *Old Nurse of the Mountains* because they didn't know of her true rank. One of Kintaro's favorite things to do was to smash stones and rocks. Just think about his strength!

Kintaro wasn't like other boys because he grew up in the mountains. Since he didn't have any other children his own age, he made friends with all of the animals. He learned how to speak their language. Little by little, all the animals grew tame around Kintaro and thought of him as their master. He would use them as messengers and servants. The ones he used the most were the hare, monkey, deer, and bear.

The bear would bring her cubs for Kintaro to play with, and when she came back to take them home, she would give Kintaro a ride on her back. Kintaro liked the deer, too. He would place his arms around these magnificent creatures' neck to show them that their horns didn't scare him. They all had a lot of fun together.

Kintaro was traveling into the mountains one day, followed by the hare, deer, monkey, and bear. After they had walked for quite a while up hills and down into the valley, over rough terrain, they came upon a grassy plain that was covered with wildflowers.

Here it was a very nice place where they could have a lot of fun together. The deer walked to a tree and began rubbing its antlers on it. The monkey scratched his back against another tree. The hare smoothed out his long ears, and the bear grunted her satisfaction.

Kintaro took in the view and stated, 'Here is a place for a good game. What do you all say to a wrestling match?'

Since the bear was the oldest and largest, she answered for everyone.

'That would be a lot of fun. I am the strongest animal, so I will make a platform for all the wrestlers.'

She began working on digging up the earth and patting it into shape.

'That looks great,' stated Kintaro. 'I will watch while you wrestle one another. I will give a prize to the one who wins in every round.'

'This will be lots of fun! We shall all try to get a prize.' stated the bear.

The hare, monkey, and deer starting working to help the bear create the platform that they were to wrestle on top of.

Once it was finished, Kintaro shouted: 'Now begin! The hare and the monkey will open this sport and the deer will be the umpire.'

'Yes,' answered the deer. 'I will be the umpire. Now, monkey and hare if you are ready, please walk up here and take you place on the platform.'

The hare and monkey both went nimbly and quickly up to the platform. Since the deer was the umpire, he stood between the two opponents and said:

'Red-back! Red-back!' because monkeys in Japan have red backs. 'Are you ready?'

He then turned to the hare. 'Long-ears! Long-ears, are you ready?'

Both of the wrestlers faced each other. The deer raised a leaf as high as he could as a signal. Once he dropped the leaf, the hare and monkey rushed toward each other saying: 'Yoisho, yoisho!'

During the time the hare and monkey were wrestling, the deer was calling out encouraging words or shouted warnings to the wrestlers if they pushed each other too close to the edge of the platform

The deer would call out every now and then: 'Red-back! Red-back! Stand your ground!'

The bear would grunt: 'Long-ears! Long-ears! Be strong, stand your ground, don't let that monkey beat you!'

So the hare and the monkey, being encouraged by their friends, tried their hardest to beat each other. The hare gained on the monkey when the monkey tripped. The hare gave him a push that sent him flying off of the platform.

Monkey sat up rubbing his back. His face was long and he angrily screamed. 'Oh, oh! How my back hurts! My back hurts me!'

Seeing that the monkey on the ground, the deer held the leaf high and declared:

'This round is finished. The hare won.'

Kintaro opened his lunch box and took out a rice dumpling and gave it to the hare. He stated 'Here is your prize, you earned it well!'

The monkey got up looking very angry and as they say in Japan 'his stomach stood up,' because he felt like he hadn't been beaten fairly. He said to his friends:

'I have not been beaten fairly. My foot slipped and I fell. Please give me another chance and let the hare wrestle with me another round.'

Kintaro consented so the monkey and hare began wrestling again. Now, everybody knows that monkeys can be very cunning and he had made up his mind to beat the hare this time if he could. In order to accomplish this, the thought the best way would be to grab the hare by his ear. He finally managed to do this. The hare was thrown off guard by the pain of getting his ear pulled hard. The monkey seized the opportunity and caught one of the hare's legs and sent him sprawling in the middle of the platform. The monkey won this round and received a rice dumpling from Kintaro. This made him very happy and he forgot about his sore back.

The deer went up to the hare and asked if he was ready for another round and if so, would he like to wrestle him. The hare consented. The stood up and got ready to wrestle. The bear stepped forward to become the umpire.

The hare with his long ears and the deer with his long antlers was a funny sight to watch. All of a sudden the deer went down on his knees and the bear declared the hare to be the winner. The little party kept wrestling and enjoying themselves until everyone was very tired.

Kintaro stood up and said:

'This is enough for today. What a nice place we have found to wrestle, let us come back tomorrow. Now we will all go home. Come along!' With this being said, Kintaro led the way with his friends following behind him.

After they had walked for a while they came out on the banks of a river that flowed through the valley. Kintaro and his friends looked around for some way for them to cross the river. There wasn't a bridge to be seen. They river rushed down in its way. All the animals looked so serious and wondered how they would be able to cross the river so they could get home.

Kintaro said, 'Wait a moment. I will make a bridge for you in a couple of minutes.' the hare, monkey, deer, and bear looked to see what he was going to do.

Kintaro went from one tree to another that was growing along the backs of the river. He at last stopped in front of a huge tree that was growing near the water's edge. He grabbed hold of the tree's trunk and pulled it hard once, twice, and then one more time to make three! When he pulled the third time, Kintaro's strength was so strong that the roots gave way and the tree fell over to create a bridge that went across the river.

'There,' said Kintaro. 'What do you think of my bridge? It is very safe, so follow me,' he stepped across with the other four animals following him. Never had they seen one person who was so strong. They all exclaimed:

'How strong he is! How strong he is!'

While all of this was happening by the river, a woodcutter who was standing on a rock that overlooked the river had seen all of this happening below him. He watched with amazement when Kintaro and his animal friends walked across the tree bridge. He actually rubbed his eyes to make sure that he wasn't dreaming when he watched this boy pull up a tree by its roots and throw it across the river to make a bridge.

The woodcutter, marveled at everything he had seen and said to himself, 'This isn't an ordinary child. Whose son could he be? I will figure this out before this day is over.'

He hurried after this strange part and crossed the river behind them. Kintaro didn't realize they were being followed. When he reached the other side of the river, he and his animals went their own separate ways.

When he entered his cottage, that looked like a little matchbox in the middle of the woods, he went to greet his mother.

'Okkasan, here I am!'

'O, Kimbo!' said his mother with a smile. She was glad to see her son home and safe after a long day. 'You are very late today. I worried that something had happened to you. Where have you been all day?'

'I took my friends, the hare, monkey, deer, and bear up into the hills and there I had them do some wrestling matches to see who was the strongest. Everyone enjoyed the sport, and we will be going to the same place tomorrow to wrestle again.'

'Well, tell me who is the strongest of all?' asked his mother as if she didn't know.

'Oh, mother, don't you know that I am the strongest? There was no need for me to wrestle with any of them.'

'Okay, but next to you, who was the strongest?'

'The bear comes next to me in strength.' Kintaro answered.

'After the bear?'

'Next to the bear it isn't easy to say who is the strongest. The hare, monkey, and deer all seem to be as strong as the other.' stated Kintaro.

All of a sudden, Kintaro and his mother were startled when they heard a voice outside. 'Listen to me little boy! The next time you go wrestling, will you take this old man with you? He would like to be a part of the fun, too.'

This voice was one from the woodcutter who had followed Kintaro from the river. He took off his shoes and entered the cottage. Kintaro and his mom were taken by surprise. They looked at this man and wondered who he was as they hadn't ever seen him before.

'Who are you?' they asked.

The woodcutter then laughed and said: 'It doesn't matter who I am but let's see who have the strongest arm... this boy or myself?'

Then Kintaro who had lived his entire life in the forest, answered the old man saying: 'We will have a try if you wish it, but you must not be angry whoever is beaten.'

The Kintaro and the woodcutter both put out their right arms and grasped each other's hands. For a long time Kintaro and the woodcutter wrestled together in this way, each one truing to bend the other's arm. The old man was very strong, and the pair were pretty evenly matched. At last the woodcutter desisted, and declared that it was a draw.

'You are a very strong child. There aren't many men who can boast of the strength I have in my right arm. I saw you on the banks of the river a couple hours age when you pulled the tree out of the ground to make a bridge across the river. I couldn't believe what I had seen so I followed you him. Your strength of arm, that I have just tried, proves that what I saw this afternoon was indeed real. When you are completely grown, you will be the strongest man of all Japan. It is a shame that you are hidden away in this wilderness.'

He then turned to Kintaro's mother: 'And you, mother, have you no thoughts of taking your child to the Capital and teaching him to carry a sword that befits a samurai.'

'You are very kind to take so much interest in my son,' replied his mother. 'But he is as you see, wild and uneducated, and I worry that it will be very hard to do what you say. Due to his wonderful strength as a baby, I hid him away in the country because he hurt anybody that came near him. I have wished that I could, one day, see my boy as a knight wearing two swords. Since we don't have any influential friends to introduce us at the Capital, I fear my hopes won't every come true.'

'You need not trouble yourself about that. To tell you the truth, I am no woodcutter! I am one of the great generals of Japan. My name is Sadamitsu, and I am a vassal of the powerful Lord Minamoto no Raiko. He ordered me to go round the country and look for boys who give promise of remarkable strength, so that they may be trained as soldiers for his army. I thought that I could best do this by assuming the disguise of a wood-cutter. By good fortune, I have thus unexpectedly come across your son. Now if you really wish him to be a samurai. I will take him and present him to the Lord Raiko as a candidate for his service. What do you say to this?'

So the kind general unfolded his plans to Kintaro's mother. As the general was talking, her heart filled with joy. She was there was a wonderful chance that her one wish would be fulfilled. Her wish was to see Kintaro as a samurai before she died.

She bowed her head to the ground and replied: 'I will entrust my son to you if you really mean what you say.'

Kintaro has been sitting by his mother and listening to what they were saying. Once his mother stopped talking he exclaimed: 'Oh, joy! I am to go with the general and one day I shall be a samurai!'

So, thus Kintaro's fate was settled. The general wanted to start for the Capital immediately and he took Kintaro with him. Kintaro's mother was very sad to see her some leave since he was all that she had left. She hid her sorrow by putting on a brave face. She knew it was the best thing for her son and she didn't want to discourage him just when he was getting started. Kintaro promised not to forget her. He told her that as soon as he was a knight wearing two swords he would build her a home and take care of her.

All of his animal friends the hare, monkey, deer, and bear asked if they could still serve him. When they found out that he was going away for good, they followed him all the way to the foot of the mountain to see him off.

'Kimbo, mind your manners and be a good boy.'

Kintaro's faithful animal friends said, 'Mr. Kintaro, we wish you good health on your travels.'

They all climbed a tree to watch him as long as they could and from this height, the watched him and his shadow as they got smaller and smaller until he was no longer in their sight.

The general Sadamitsu walked while rejoicing at having found a prodigy like Kintaro. When they finally arrived at their destination, the general took Kintaro straight to Lord Raiko and told him about Kintaro and how he had found him. Lord Raiko was very happy with the story. He commanded Kintaro to be brought before him. He made Kintaro one of his vassals immediately.

Lord Raiko's army was very famous for its band that was known as *The Four Braves*. These warriors were chosen specifically by the Lord from the strongest and bravest soldiers. This well-picked, small band was known throughout all of Japan because these were the bravest of all the men.

Once Kintaro had grown into a man, his master made him Chief of the *Four Braves*. He was the strongest of all of them. Right after this happened, word was brought into the city that a cannibal monster had moved in not too far away and was scaring all of the people. Lord Raiko ordered Kintaro to rescue the people. He was delighted at being able to try out his sword.

Kintaro surprised the monster at its den, he quickly cut off the monster's head that he carried back to show he had won against the monster.

Kintaro rose to be the greatest hero in Japan. His power, wealth, and honor was extremely great. He kept his promise to his mother and built her a fine house. She lived happily with him in the Capital for the rest of her life."

CHAPTER 15

The Luminous Princess – Kaguya Hime

"A long time ago, there once lived a bamboo cutter. He was very old, poor, and sad because he didn't have any children. He was worried that he would have to continue cutting bamboo until the day he died. Each morning he went into the hills, woods, or wherever he could find some bamboo to cut. Once he had decided where he wanted to cut, he would cut down those 'feathers of the forest' and then split them lengthwise or he would cut them at their joints. He would then carry the bamboo home and turn it into things he needed for the house and the things he didn't need he would sell to get some money for other things.

One morning he found a nice clump of bamboo and went to work cutting some of them down. All of a sudden, the grove of bamboo was flooded with a soft, bright light. It was like the full moon had risen right over where he was standing. He looked around astonished and saw that the light was coming out of one bamboo. The old man was filled with wander and dropped his ax. He walked slowly toward the light. As he got closer, he realized that this bright lift was coming out of a hollow in one of the stems of bamboo. What was more wonderful was in the middle of all that brilliance was a tiny little girl. She only stood about three inches high and was exquisitely beautiful.

'You must have been sent to be my child, for I find you here among the bamboos where lies my daily work.' The old man stated. He reached out and took the tiny girl in his hand. He carried her home for his wife to bring up as their own. The little girl was so beautiful and small that the old woman placed her into a basket to keep her safe from harm

The couple were very happy, for they have lived a life-time of regret since they didn't have any children of their own. They now gave the tiny girl all their love because she had come to time in such a great way.

From then on, while the old man was cutting down the bamboo and cutting it into pieces, he would sometimes find gold inside some of the bamboo. There were times when he found precious stones inside the bamboo, too. Little by little, he became rich. He built his family a very fine house and they weren't known as the poor woodcutter and his wife anymore since he was a very wealthy man.

Three months went by very fast and during that time the tiny girl has grown into a full size girl. Her foster parents fixed her hair and dressed her in the most beautiful kimonos. She was so beautiful that the put her behind a screen like a princess. They didn't allow anyone to see her and they waited on her just like she was a real princess. It was almost like she was made from light because their house would be filled with a soft, shining, essence so that even during the darkest of nights were like daytime. Her presence have a wonderful influence on the people around her, too. Anytime the man felt sad, he just had to look at his beautiful dauther and his sadness vanished immediately. He was as happy as he had been when he was a lot younger.

The day finally came when the decided to name their child, they called in the best name-giver and he gave her the name of Princess Moonlight. She was named this because her body gave off so much soft light that she could have been the Moon God's daughter.

For three days this festival continued with music, dancing, and songs. All the couples family and friends were there celebrating with them. Everyone was enjoying the celebration of Princess Moonlight being named. Everybody who saw her said that they had never been another person who was as lovely. Any of the other beautiful maidens throughout the land would pale in comparison to her. The fame of her beauty spread far and wide. There were many suitors who wanted to look upon her beauty and others wanted her hand in marriage.

Suitors from all over positioned themselves outside her house. They make small holes in the fence hoping to just see her for a moment as she went from room to room. They remained at their posts day and night and sacrificed sleep just for a chance to see her but this was all done in vain. They would approach the house and even tried to speak to her parents or one of the servants but nothing was granted to them.

Despite all of their disappointment, they remained there day after day, night after night, and didn't even think anything about it. This was how great their desire was just to see the Princess.

Finally, most of the men noticed how hopeless their quest was lost hope and heart and went back to their homes. Everyone left except five knights, whose determination and ardor rather than waning seemed to grow more when faced with obstacles. These men went without eating and took small bites on anything that was brought to them so they could always be outside her house. They remained standing in all kinds of weather.

They would sometimes write letters to the Princess, but nobody ever answered any of them. When the letters failed to get any replies, they began writing poems telling her how hopelessly in love they were with her and how they couldn't sleep, eat, rest, or go home. But Princess Moonlight never acknowledged having received any of their letters.

Winter came along and still the men remained outside the Princess' home. The snow, frost, and cold slowly gave way to the warmth of spring. Then summer came around. The sun burned scorching and white in the heavens and on earth. Those faithful Knights continued watching and waiting. At the end of these long months, they called out to the bamboo-cutter and asked him to have mercy of them and to allow them to see the Princess. His only answer was that he wasn't her true father and couldn't insist on her obeying him if she didn't want to.

After the five knights heard this stern answer, they went back to their various homes and worried about what they could do to touch the Princess's heart or even have a hearing granted. They picked up their rosaries and knelt before they altars in their homes, they burned incense, and prayed to Buddha to give them what their hearts desired. Several days passes but none of them could rest in their homes.

Once again they began walking to the bamboo -cutter's house but this time the old man met them outside. They asked him to tell them if it was the Princess's wish to never see any man ever. They asked him to speak for them and to tell her about their love for her. They asked him to tell her how long they had waited throught the heat of summer, cold of winter, roofless, and sleepless without rest of food in the hopes of winner her heart. They were willing to think of this vigil as pleasure if she could just give them a chance to plead their cause.

The old man listened carefully to their tale of love and he really felt sorry for these suitors who were so faithful to his foster-daughter. He would really like to see his foster-daughter married to one of these young men. He decided to talk with Princess Moonlight.

He spoke to her very reverently: 'Although you have always seemed to me to be a heavenly being, yet I have had the trouble of bringing you up as my own child and you have been glad of the protection of my roof. Will you refuse to do as I wish?'

Princess Moonlight then replied that there wasn't anything that she wouldn't do for him. She loved and honored him as if he were her own father. She could not remember a time before she came to earth.

The bamboo-cutter listened with joy as she spoke these words. He then told her how anxious he was to see her happily and safely married before he died.

'I am an old man, over 70 years of age, and my end may come any time now. It is necessary and right that you should see these five suitors and choose one of them.'

'Oh, why must I do this? I have no wish to marry now.' replied the Princess in distress.

'I found you many years ago, when you were just a tiny creature and only stood three inches high. You were standing in the middle of a great white light. The light streamed from the bamboo in which you were hid and led me to you. So I have always thought that you were more than a mortal woman. While I am alive it is right for you to remain as you are if you wish to do so, but someday I shall cease to be and who will take care of you then? Therefore I pray you to meet these five brave men one at a time and make up your mind to marry one of them.'

The Princess them answered that she felt sure she wasn't as beautiful as they thought she was and even if she did agree to marry one of them without knowing her before, his heart might change later. Since she didn't feel sure of any of them, and even though her father has told her that they were worthy Knights, she didn't feel like she should see them.

'All that you say is very reasonable, but what kind of men will you consent to see? I do not call these five men who have waited on you for years, light-hearted. They have stood outside this house through the entire summer and winter. They have denied themselves sleep and food so they might catch a glimpse of you. What more could you demand of them?' the old man asked.

Princess Moonlight said she had to make sure of their love before she would grant their request to speak with her. The five knights had to prove their love by bringing her something that she wanted from a distant country.

That evening the five knights came to her house and started playing their flutes for her. They sang songs that they had composed telling about their tireless and great love. The bamboo-cutter went out and offered them some sympathy for everything they had went through and the patience they had shown when trying to win the Princess's heart. He gave them her message that she would marry whosoever could bring her the things she wanted from distant countries. This was her test for them."

CHAPTER 16

The Mirror of Matsuyama

"A long time ago in ancient Japan, in the Province of Echigo, which is a very remote area of Japan even for those days, there lived a man and his wife. They had been married for a long time and had been blessed with a daughter. She was their pride and joy and she gave them endless happiness. They stored as much of this happiness inside them to get them through their old age.

They held wonderful memories from her childhood like her first visit to the temple when she was a month old. They remembered her mother carrying her in her ceremonial kimono to be placed under the patronage of the family's god. Then was the memory of her first doll festival when her parents gave her a doll set and all their tiny belongings. They added to this every years and the most important day was on her third birthday when they tied her first OBI of gold and scarlet around her waist. This showed she had crossed into girlhood and had left infancy behind her. Now she was seven years old and had been walking and talking for many years. He had learned to wait on her parents in her short time on earth and this just make her parents even happier. There wasn't a family in all the lad that was as happy as this one.

One day, there was a lot of excitement in their home, for the father had been summoned to the capital for business. In these days of junrickshas and railways and other ways of rapid traveling, it was hard to realize what kind of journey he had from Matsuyama to Kyoto. The roads back then were bad and rough and people had to walk everywhere they went. It didn't matter if the distance was one mile or several hundred miles. During these days, it was a great undertaking to go to the capital just like it would be to travel from Japan to Europe now.

His wife was very anxious while she was helping her husband get ready fro his long journey. She knew that he had a hard task in front of him. She vainly wished that she could go with him, but the distance was too much for a mother and a small child to travel and she had to take care of the house as was her duty.

Everything was finally ready and the husband stood on the porch with his family around him.

'Do not be anxious. I will come back as soon as I can.' he said. 'While I am away take care of everything, and especially our little daughter.'

'Yes. We shall be all right, but you, you mucht take care of yourself and don't delay even for one day of coming back to us.' said his wife, while her tears fell like rain.

The small girl was the only one to smile, for she didn't completely understand how sad partings could be, and did not realize that traveling to the capital was different than just walking to the next village and her father did that a lot. She ran to him and took hold of his sleeve to get his attention.

'Father, I will be very good while I am waiting for you to come home, so please bring me a present.'

As her father turned to take one more look at his crying wife and smiling daughter, he felt like somebody was pulling him back by his hair. It was so intense that it was hard for him to leave them because they hadn't ever been separated before. He knew he had to go, for the call was very important. With all his might he stopped thinking and turned away. He traveled quickly down past their little garden and out through the gate. Her wife picked up their child and ran to the gate. They watched him as he traveled down the road between the pines until he was only a haze in the distance and all she could see was his peaked hat and it soon vanished, too.

EBISU, THE FISH-GOD OF JAPAN, HOLDING A RED TAI

'Now father has gone, you and I must take care of everything until he comes back.' said the mother, as she walked back to their house.

'Yes, I will be very good.' said the little girl, nodding her head. 'And when father comes home please tell him how good I had been, and then perhaps he will give me present.'

'Father is sure to bring you something that you want very much. I know, for I asked him to bring you a doll. You must think of father every day, and pray for a safe journey until he comes back.'

'Oh, yes, when he comes home again how happy I shall be.' said the small child, clapping her hands, and her face grew bright with joy at the happy thoughts. I seemed to her mother as she looked at her daughter's face that her love for her only grew deeper.

She then started making their winter clothes. She set up her wooden spinning wheel and spun all the thread before she started to weave the cloth. During any time that she wasn't weaving, she would direct her daughter's games and taught her to read all the old stories. This is how the wife found peace while working during her lonely days while her husband was away. Even though the time was going quickly by in their quiet home, the husband finally finished his work and returned home.

It would have been hard for anyone who didn't know the man to even recognize him. He had traveled every day being exposed to all sorts of weather for one month. He had been sunburnt until his skin was now a bronze color, but his wife and daughter knew him in an instant. They ran to meet him one on each side of him. The mother and daughter worked together to untie his sandals, take off his large umbrella hat until he was comfortable again in the middle of their sitting room that had once been very empty while he was gone.

Once they had sat down on the white mats, the man opened the bamboo basket that he had taken with him and he took out a beautiful doo and a box full of cakes.

'Here,' he said to his daughter, 'is a present for you. It is a prize for taking are of mother and the house so well while I was gone.'

'Thank you,' said the child, as she bowed her head to the ground and then put out her hand like a maple leaf with her fingers spread wide to take the doll and the box of cakes that came from the capital. Both were prettier than anything she had ever seen before. There weren't any words that could describe how delighted the small child was as her face seemed like it would melt with joy, and she didn't have any thoughts for anything else.

The husband once again dove into the basket and brought out a wooden box that was square and had been tied up careful with a white and red string. He handed it to his wife and said:

'And this is for you.'

His wife took the box, and opened it carefully. She took out a metal disk that had a handle attached. One side was shiny and bright like a crystal while the other side was covered with raised figures of storks and pine trees. These had been carved into the smooth surface. She hadn't ever seen anything like this in her life. She had been born and raised in the rural province of Echigo. She looked into the shiny side and looked up in surprise and wonder at her face.

'I see someone looking at me in this round thing! What is it that you have given to me?'

Her husband laughed and said, 'Why, it is your own face that you see. What I have brought you is called a mirror, and whoever looks into its clear surface can see their won face reflected there. Even though there aren't any that can be found in this place but they are used in the capital from ancient times. In the capital, the mirror is considered a necessary requisite for any woman to have. There is an old proverb that states: *As the sword is the soul of a samurai, so is the mirror the soul of a woman*, and according to tradition, a woman's mirror is an index to her own heart as long as she keeps it bright and clear, so is her heart pure and good. It is also one of the treasures that form the insignia of the Emperor. So you must lay great store by your mirror and use it carefully.'

The wife listened to all that her husband told her, and was pleased to learn so much that was new to her. She was still more pleased at the precious gift. His token of remembrance while he was away.

'If the mirror represents my soul, I shall certainly treasure it as a valuable possession, and never will I use it carelessly.' As she said this, she lifted up to her forehead, to show gratitude for the gift, she then put it in her box and put it away.

The wife say that her husband was very tired, and started fixing the evening meal and making everything as comfortable as she could for him. It seemed to this little family that they hadn't know what true happiness was until now, since they were so happy to be together again. One this evening, the father has a lot ot tell about his journey and of all the things he had seen in the capital.

Time passed peacefully in their little home and the parents saw their hopes realized as their daughter grew out of childhood and into a beautiful maiden at the age of 16. Just like any priceless gem holds value for its owner, so had they brought her up with unceasing care and love and their pains had been rewarded. She was a great comfort to her mother as she took up part of the housekeeping. Her father was very proud of her for she reminded him of her mother when they had been first married.

But as we know, nothing lasts forever. Even the moon doesn't keep it shape all the time. The flowers bloom will soon fade away, too. The happiness of this family was broken by a great sorrow. The gentle and good wife was taken ill one day.

During the first days of her illness, the daughter and father thought it was just a cold and weren't all the worried. But as the days went by and the mother wasn't getting any better. She just grew worse and worse. The doctor was confused because all the he did, the mother just got weaker and weaker each day. The daughter and father were full of grief and day and night the girl never left her mother's side. In spite of all their efforts the woman's life was not to be saved.

One day as the girl sat near her mother, trying to hide her sorrow with a cheery smile, the mother woke up briefly and took her daughter's hand. She gazed lovingly and earnestly into her eyes. Her breath was labored and it was hard for her to talk.

'My daughter, I am sure that nothing can save me now. When I am dead, promise me that you will take care of your father and try to be a good and dutiful woman.'

'Oh, mother,' said the girl as tears streamed down her face. 'You must not say such things. All you have to do is to make hast and get will as this will bring the greatest happiness to myself and father.'

'Yes, I know, and it is a comfort to me in my last days to know how greatly you long for me to get better, but it is not to be. Do not look so sorrowful, for it was so ordained in my previous state of existence that I should die in this life just at this time, knowing this, I am quite resigned to my fate. And now I have something to give you whereby to remember me when I am gone.'

Putting her hand out, she took from the side of the pillow a square wooden box tied with a silken cord and tassels. Undoing it carefully, she took out the box that held the mirror her husband had given to her years ago.

'When you were still a small child, your father went to the capital and brought me back this treasure as a present. This is a mirror. This I give to you before I die. If, after I have ceased to be in this life, you are longly and long to see me, then take out this mirror and in the shiny, clear surface, you will always see me. You will be able to meet with me often and tell me all your heart. Even though I shall not be able to speak, I shall understand and sympathize with you whatever might happen to you in the future.' With these words, the dying woman handed the mirror to her daughter.

The mother's mind seemed to be a rest now and she sank back into the pillow without another word and her spirit passed quietly away later that day.

The bereaved daughter and father were crazy with grief and they abandoned themselves to their sorrow. They felt that it was impossible to take leave of the woman they loved who until now had filled their entire lives and commit her body into the ground. This horrific burst of grief passed, and then they took possession of their hearts again, even though their hearts were crushed, they now resigned themselves to their lives.

The daughter's life seemed so be so desolate. Her love for her mother didn't grow any less over time, and she remembered her mother so keenly. Everything in her life, even the falling rain and blowing wind reminded her of her mother's death and of all the love they had shared. One day while her father was out, and she was doing her household chores, her sorrow and loneliness seemed more than she could bear. She threw herself down in her mother's room and wept as if her heart were breaking all over again. The poor child was longing for one more glimpse of her mother's lovely face, one sound of her mother's voice calling her by her nickname, or for one moment of forgetfulness of this aching void in her heart. She suddenly sat up as her mother's last words rang through her memory and dulled her grief.

'Oh! My mother told me when she gave me the mirror as a parting gift, that whenever I looked into it I should be able to meet her, to see her. I had nearly forgotten her last words; how stupid I am. I will get the mirror now and see if it can possibly be true!'

She quickly dried her eyes, and going to the cupboard, took out the box that contained the mirror, her heart was beating with expectation as she lifted the mirror out and gazed into its smooth face. Behold, her mother's words were true! In the round mirror before her she saw her mother's face, but, oh, the joyful surprise! It wasn't her mother's thin and wasted face but they beautiful and young woman that she remembered from her youth. It seemed to the girl that the face in the mirror must speak, almost that she heard her mother's voice telling her again to grow up to be a dutiful daughter and good woman, so earnestly did the eyes in the mirror look back into her own.

'It is certainly my mother's soul that I see. She knows how miserable I am without her and she has come to comfort me. Whenever I long to see her she will meet me here, how grateful I ought to be!'

And from this time, their weight of sorrow was greatly lightened for her young heart. Every morning, to gather her strength for the day ahead of her, and each evening, to console her before she laid down to rest, the young girl took out the mirror and gazed at the reflection that she thought was her mother's soul. Each day she grew more and more to look like her dead mother and she was kind and gentle and all. She was a very dutiful daughter to her father.

A year of mourning has passed through this house, when, on the advice of his relatives, the man decided to marry again. The daughter was now under the authority of her stepmother. It was a hard position for her but she spent her days thinking about her own loving mother. She tried to be what her mother wanted her to be and this caused her to be patient and docile and she was now determined to be faithful and dutiful to her stepmother in every aspect. Everything went so smooth for the family for quite some time. There weren't any waves or winds of discord in their daily lives that the father became very content.

It is a woman's heart to be mean and petty and since stepmothers are all over the world, this one's heart was not the same as her fake smiles were. As the days grew into weeks and the weeks grew into months, the stepmother began to treat the daughter unkindly and she tried to come between the child and her father.

There were times when she would go to her husband and complain about the way her stepdaughter was treating her, but the father knew that this was normal and he didn't take notice of her complaints. Rather than lessening his affection for his daughter like she wanted, her grumblings only made him think more of her. The woman soon realized that he was starting to show more concern for his child more and more. This didn't please her at all and she started thinking about how she could get her stepdaughter out of her house. This is how evil her heart had turned.

She watched her stepdaughter carefully, and she peeked into her room one evening and thought she had discovered a horrible sin that she could accuse the child of to her father. The woman herself was a bit frightened at what she had seen.

She went at once to her husband, and wiped at some false tears, she said in a very sad voice:

'Please give me permission to leave you today.'

The man was totally take by surprise at her request as it was so sudden and wondered what had happened.

'Do you find it so disagreeable in my house that you can stay no longer?' he asked.

'No! No! It have nothing to do with you. Even in my dreams I have never thought that I wished to leave your side, but if I go on living here I am in danger of losing my life, so I think it best for all concerned that you should allow me to go home!'

The woman started crying again and this make her husband distressed to see her so unhappy. He thought surely that he hadn't heard her right and said:

'Tell me what you mean! How is your life in danger here?'

'I will tell you since you ask me. Your daughter dislikes me as her step-mother. For some time past, she has shut herself up in her room morning and evening, and looking in as I passed by, I am convinced that she had made an image of me and is trying to kill me by magic, cursing me daily. It is not safe for me to stay here, such being the case. Indeed! Indeed! I must go away, we cannot live under the same roof anymore.'

The husband listened to this dreadful tale, but he could not believe his gentle daughter guilty of such an evil act. He knew that by popular superstition people believed that one person could cause the gradual death of another by making an image of the hated one and cursing it daily; but where had his young daughter learned such knowledge? This kind of thing was impossible. Yet he remembered having noticed that his daughter stayed much of the time in her room of late and kept herself away from everyone, even when they had visitors at the house. Putting all these facts together with his wife's accusation, he thought that there may be something to account for the strange story.

His heart became torn between him trusting his child and his doubting wife and he didn't know what he should do. He decided to go to his daughter and see if he could figure out the truth. He comforted his wife and assured her that her fears were completely groundless. He slid quietly into his daughter's room.

The girl had been unhappy for a very long time. She had tried to be nice and obedient to show her goodwill and to appease her father's new wife. She had tried to break down the wall of misunderstanding and prejudice that she knew usually stood between step-parents and their step-children. She soon found that all her efforts were in vain. Her stepmother never trusted her, and seemed to misinterpret all her actions. The poor child knew very well that she carried all sorts of untrue and unkind tales to her father. She couldn't help comparing her present unhappy state to the time when her mother was alive just over a year ago. So much had changed in such a short time. Each morning and each evening, she wept when she remembered. Whenever she could, she would go to her room, and sliding the door shut, she would take out the mirror and look while she thought about her mother's face. It was the only joy she had during these horrible days.

Her father found her gazing into the mirror. He pushed aside the door and saw her bent over something very intently. She looked over her shoulder to see who had entered her room; the girl was surprised to see her father, for he normally would send for her if he wanted to speak with her. She was so confused with being found looking into the mirror, as she had never told anybody about her mother's promise, but had kept this secret in her heart. Before she turned to her father, she slipped the mirror into her sleeve. Her father noticed her confusion and her hiding something and he said in a severe manner:

'Daughter, what are you doing here? And what is that you have hidden in your sleeve?'

The girl became scared by the severity of her father's voice. He had never spoken to her in a tone like this. Her confusion changed into apprehension, her color went from scarlet to white. She sat shamefaced and dumb. She was not able to reply.

Appearances were certainly against her, the young girl did look very guilty, and her father thought that perhaps after all that his wife had told him was very true so he spoke angrily at his daughter:

'Then, is it really true that you are daily cursing your stepmother and praying for her death? Have you forgotten what I told you, that although she is your stepmother you must be obedient and loyal to her? What evil spirit has taken possession of your heart that you should be so wicked? You have certainly changed my

daughter! What has made you so disobedient and un-
faithful?'

And her father's eyes filled with tears to think that he
should have to upbraid his daughter in this way. She on
her part didn't know what he meant, for she had never
heard of the superstition that by praying over an image
it is possible to cause the death of a hated person. But
she saw that she must speak and clear herself somehow.
She loved her father dearly, and couldn't bear the idea
of his anger. She put out her hand on his knee lovingly.

'Father! Father! Do not say such dreadful things to me.
I am still your obedient child. Indeed, I am. However
stupid I may be, I should never be able to curse anyone
who belonged to you, much less pray for the death of
one you love. Surely someone has been telling you lies,
and you are dazed, and you know now what you say or
some evil spirit has taken possession of YOUR heart.
As for me I do not know, no, not so much as a dew drop
of the evil thing that you accuse me of.'

But the father remembered that she had hidden something away when he came into the room and even this
protest didn't satisfy him. He wished to clear up his
doubts once and for all.

'Then why are you always alone in your room these days? And tell me what is that you have hidden in your sleeve. Show it to me at once.'

Then the daughter, though shy of confessing how she had cherished her mother's memory, saw that she must tell her father all in order to clear herself. So she slipped the mirror out from her long sleeve and laid it before him.

'This is what you saw me looking at just now.' she told him.

'Why, this is the mirror that I brought as a gift to your mother when I went up to the capital many, many years ago! And you have kept it all this time? Now, why do you spend so much of your time before this mirror?'

Then she told him of her mother's last words, and of how she had promised to meet her child whenever she looked into the glass. But still the father could not understand the simplicity of his daughter's character in not knowing that what she saw reflected in the mirror was in reality her own face, and not that of her mother.

'What do you mean?' he asked. 'I don't understand how you can meet the soul of your lost mother by looking in this mirror?'

'It is indeed true,' said the girl. 'And if you don't believe what I say, look for yourself.' She placed the mirror before her. There, looking back from the smooth surface was her own sweet face. She pointed to the reflection seriously.

'Do you still doubt me?' she asked him earnestly, looking into his face.

With an exclamation of sudden understanding, her father smacked his hands together.

'How stupid I am! At last I understand. Your face is as like your mother's as the two sides of a melon. Thus you have looked at the reflection of your face all this time, thinking that you were brought face to face with your lost mother! You are truly a faithful child. It seems at first a stupid thing to have done, but it is not really so. It shows how deep has been your faithfulness and how innocent your heart. Living in constant remembrance of you mother has helped you to grow like her in character. How clever it was of her to tell you to do this. I admire and respect you, my daughter, and I am ashamed to think that for one instant that I believed your suspicious stepmother's story and suspected you of evil, and came with the intention of scolding you severely, while all this time you have been so true and good. Before you I have no countenance left, and I beg you to forgive me.'

And here the father wept. He thought of how lonely the poor girl must have been, and of all that she must have suffered under her stepmother's treatment. His daughter steadfastly kept her faith and simplicity in the midst of such adverse circumstances, bearing all her troubles with so much patience and goodness. This made him compare her to the lotus which rears its blossoms of dazzling beauty out of the mud and slime of the moats and ponds, fitting emblem of a heart which keeps itself unsullied while passing through the world.

The stepmother, anxious to know what would happen, had all this while been standing outside the room. She had grown interested, and had slowing pushed the door back until she could see all that was happening. At this moment, she entered the room and dropped to the mats, she bowed her head over her outspread hands before her stepdaughter.

'I am ashamed! I am ashamed!' she exclaimed. 'I didn't know what a faithful child you were. Through no fault of your, but what a stepmother's jealous heart. I have disliked you all this time. Hating you so much myself, it was but natural that I should think you reciprocated that feeling. And thus when I say you retire so often to your room, I followed you, and when I say you gazing into the mirror daily for such a long time, I concluded that you had found out how much I disliked you and you were trying to get revenge by taking my life by magic. As long as I live, I shall never forget the wrong I have done you in misjudging you, and in causing your father to suspect you. From this day, I throw away my old and wicked heart, and in its place I put a new one, clean and full of repentance. I shall think of you as a child that I have borne myself. I shall love and cherish you with all my heart, and thus try to make up for all the unhappiness I have caused you. Therefore, please throw into the water all that has gone before, and give me. I beg of you, some of the faithful love that you have hitherto given to your own lost mother.'

Thus did the unkind stepmother humble herself and ask forgiveness of the girl that she had so wronged.

Such was the sweetness of the girl's disposition that she willingly forgave her stepmother, and never bore a moment's resentment or malice towards her afterwards. The father saw by his wife's face that she was truly sorry for the past, and was greatly relieved to see the terrible misunderstanding wiped out of remembrance by both the wrong-doer and the wronged.

From this time on, the three lived together as happily as fish in water. No such trouble ever darkened the home again, and the young girl gradually forgot that year of unhappiness in the tender love and care that her stepmother now bestowed on her. Her patience and goodness were rewarded at last."

CHAPTER 17

The Jelly Fish and The Monkey

"A long time ago, in old Japan, the Kingdom of the Sea was rule by an amazing King. He was known as Ryn Jin, or the Dragon King of the Sea. His power was immense, for he was the rule of all sea creatures both great and small. He also held the Jewels of the Ebb and Flow of the Tide. The Jewel of the Ebbing Tide would cause the sea to recede from the land, and the Jewel of the Flowering Tide made the waves rise mountains high and flow onto the shore like a tidal wave.

The Palace of Ryn Jin was located at the bottom of the sea, and was so beautiful that no one had even seen anything like it, even in their dreams. The walls were of coral, the roof of chryosprase and jadestone, and the floors were of the finest mother-of-pearl. But the Dragon King, in spite of his wide-spreading Kingdom, his beautiful Palace and all of its wonders, and his power which none disputes throughout the whole sea, was not at all happy, for he reigned alone. He felt that if he married, he would not only be happier, but also more powerful. He decided to take a wife. Calling all his fish together, he chose several of them as ambassadors to go through the sea and seek out a young Dragon Princess who would be his bride.

They finally returned to the Palace, and with them they had a lovely young dragon. Her scales glittered with green like the wings of summer beetles. Her eyes threw out glances of fire, and she was dressed in gorgeous robes. All of the jewels of the sea were embroidered on her clothing.

It was love at first sight for the King, and the wedding ceremony was celebrated with great splendor. Every living thing within the sea, from the great whales down to the little shrimps, came in schools to offer their congratulations to the bride and groom, and to wish them a long and happy life together. Never had there been such an assemblage or such a happy event in the Fish-World before. The train of bearers who carried the bride's possessions to her new home seemed to reach across the waves from one end of sea to the other. Every single fish carried a phosphorescent lantern and was dressed in ceremonial robes, gleaming in pink, blue, and sliver. All of the waves that rose, fell, and broke that night seemed to be rolling masses of green and white fire, for the phosphorus shone with double brilliancy in honor of the event.

Now, for some time, the Dragon King and his bride lived very happily. They loved each other dearly, and the groom, day after day, took delight in showing his bride all of the treasures and wonders of his coral Palace, and she was never tired of wandering with him through its vast gardens and halls. Their life together seemed like a long summer's day.

Two months passed in this happy way, and suddenly the Dragon Queen fell ill and was forced to stay in bed. The King was overcome with emotions when he saw his precious bride so ill, and at once sent for the fish doctor to come and treat her. He gave special orders to the servants to nurse her carefully and to wait upon her with diligence, but in spite of all the nurses' care and the medicine that the doctor prescribed, the young Queen showed no signs of recovery. Each day, she continued to grow sicker.

Then the Dragon King interviewed the doctor and blamed him for not curing the Queen. The doctor was alarmed at Ryn Jin's unhappiness, and excused his want of skill by saying that although he knew the right kind of medicine to give the invalid, it was impossible to find it in the sea.

'Do you mean to tell me that you can't get the medicine here?' asked the Dragon King.

'It is just as you say!' and the doctor.

'Tell me what it is you want for the Queen?' demanded Ryn Jin.

'I want the liver of a live monkey!' answered the doctor.

'The liver of a live money! Of course that will be most difficult to get,' said the King.

'If we could only get that for the Queens, Her Majesty would soon recover,' said the doctor.

'Very well, that decides it. We MUST get it somehow or other. But where are we most likely to find a monkey?' asked the King.

The doctor then told the Dragon King that some distance to the south there was a Monkey Island where a great number of monkey's resided.

'If only you could capture one of these monkeys,' said the doctor.

'How can any of my people capture a monkey?' said the Dragon King, greatly puzzled. 'The monkeys live on dry land, while we live in the water, and out of our element we are quite powerless! I don't see what we can do.'

'That has been my difficulty too,' said the doctor. 'But amongst your innumerable servants, you surely can find one who can go on shore for that express purpose.'

'Something must be done.' The called in his chief steward he consulted in all matters.

The chief steward thought for some time, and then, as if struck by a sudden though, said joyfully, 'I know what we must do. There is a jellyfish. He is certainly ugly to look at, but he is proud of being able to walk on land with his four legs like a tortoise. Let us send him to the Island of Monkeys to catch one.'

The jellyfish was summoned by the King, and was told by His Majesty what was required of him. The jellyfish, after being told of his unexpected mission, looked quite troubled, and said that he had never been to the island in question, and as he had never had any experience in catching monkeys, he was afraid that he would not be able to get one.

'Well,' said the chief steward, 'if you depend on your strength or dexterity you will never catch a monkey. The only way is to play a trick on one.'

'How can I play a trick on a monkey? I don't know how to do it,' said the perplexed jellyfish.

'This is what you must do,' said the chief steward. 'When you approach the Island of Monkeys and meet some of them, you must try to get very friendly with one. Tell him that you are a servant of the Dragon King, and invite him to come and visit you and see the Dragon King's Palace. Try and describe to him as vividly as you can the grandeur of the Palace and the wonders of the sea so as to arouse his curiosity and make him long to see it all!'

'But how am I to get the monkey here? You know monkeys don't swim.' Said the reluctant jellyfish.

'You will have to carry him on your back. What is the use of your shell if you can't do that,' said the chief steward.

'Won't he be very heavy?'

'You mustn't mind that, for you are working for the Dragon King,' the chief steward stated.

'I will do my best then,' said the jellyfish, and he swam away from the Palace and started off towards the Monkey Island. As he swam swiftly, he was able to reach his destination in only a few hours. He landed by a convenient wave upon the shore. Once he looked around, he saw not far away was a big pine tree with drooping branches and on one of those branches was just what he was looking for. A living and breathing monkey.

'I'm in luck,' thought the jellyfish. 'Now I must flatter the creature and try to entice him to come back with me to the Palace, and my part will be done.'

The jellyfish slowly walked towards the pine tree. In those ancient days, the jellyfish had four legs and a hard shell, just like a tortoise. When he reached the pine tree, he raised his voice and said,

'How do you do, Mr. Monkey? Isn't it a lovely day?'

'A very fine day,' answered the monkey from the tree. 'I have never seen you in this part of the world before. Where have you come from and what is your name?'

'My name is kurage or jellyfish. I am one of the servants of the Dragon King. I have heard many stories about your beautiful island that I have come on purpose to see it,' answered the jellyfish.

'I am very glad to see you,' said the monkey.

'Incidentally,' said the jellyfish, 'have you ever visited the Palace of the Dragon King of the Sea where I live?'

'I have often heard of it, but I have never seen it,' the monkey answered.

'Then you most definitely need to come visit. It is such a great pity for you to go through life without seeing it. The beauty of the Palace is beyond all description. It is certainly to my mind the most lovely place in all of the world,' said the jelly fish.

'Is it so beautiful as all that?' asked the monkey in astonishment.

Then the jellyfish saw his chance, and went on describing to the best of his ability, the beauty and grandeur of the Sea King's Palace, and the wonders of the garden with its curious trees of white, red, and pink coral, and the still more curious fruits like great jewels hanging on the branches. The monkey grew more and more interested, and as he listened, he came out of the tree branch by branch so as not to lose a word of the wonderful story.

'I have got him at last!' thought the jellyfish, but aloud he said,

'Mr. Monkey, I must not go back. As you have never seen the Palace of the Dragon King, won't you take advantage of this moment to get to see all of the splendor of the Palace with me? I shall then be able to act as guide and show you all the sights of the sea, which will be even more wonderful to you, a land-lubber.'

'I should love to go,' said the monkey, 'but how am I to cross the water. I can't swim as you surely know.'

'There is no difficulty about that. I can carry you on my back.' 'That will be troubling you too much,' said the monkey.

'I can do it quite easily. I am stronger than I look, so you needn't hesitate,' said the jellyfish, and taking the monkey on his back, he stepped into the sea.

'Keep very still, Mr. Monkey,' said the jellyfish. 'You mustn't fall into the sea. I am responsible for your safe arrival at the King's Palace.'

'Please don't go so fast, or I am sure I shall fall off,' said the monkey.

As such, they traveled along. The jellyfish skimmed through the waves with the monkey balancing on his back. When they were about halfway, the jellyfish, who knew very little about anatomy, began to wonder if the monkey had his liver with him or not.

'Mr. Monkey, tell me, have you such a thing as a liver with you?'

The monkey was taken aback by such an odd question, and asked what the jellyfish wanted with a liver.

'That is the most important thing of all,' said the stupid jellyfish, 'so as soon as I recollected it, I asked you if you had yours with you.'

'Why is my liver so important to you?' asked the monkey.

'Oh, you will learn the reason later,' said the jellyfish.

The monkey became more and more suspicious and curious, and urged the jellyfish to tell him for what his liver was wanted, and appealed to his hearer's feeling by saying that he was extremely troubled at what he had been told. Then, the jellyfish, seeing how anxious the monkey looked, was sorry for him, and told him everything. How the Dragon Queen had fallen ill, and how the doctor had said that only the liver of a live monkey would cure her, and how the Dragon King had sent him to find one.

'Now I have done as I was told, and as soon as we arrive at the Palace, the doctor will want your liver, so I feel sorry for you!' said the silly jellyfish.

The poor monkey was horrified when he learnt all of this, and very angry at the trick played upon him. He trembled with fear at the thought of what was in store for him. But the monkey was a very clever animal, and he thought it the wisest plan not to show any sign of the fear he felt, so he tried to calm himself to think of some way by which he might escape.

'The doctor means to cut me open and then take my liver out! Why I shall die!' thought the monkey. A last a bright idea came to his mind, so he said quite cheerfully to the jellyfish, 'What a pity it was, Mr. Jellyfish, that you did not speak of this before we left the island!'

'If I had told why I wanted you to accompany me you would certainly have refused to come,' answered the jellyfish.

'You are quite mistaken,' said the monkey. 'Monkeys can very well spare a liver or two, especially when it is wanted for the Dragon Queen of the Sea. If I had only guessed of what you were in need, I should have presented you with one without waiting to be asked. I have several livers, but the greatest pity is that as you did not speak in time, I have left all of my livers hanging on the pine tree.'

'Have you left your liver behind you?' asked the jellyfish.

'Yes,' said the cunning monkey, 'during the daytime I usually leave my liver hanging on the branch in a tree, as it is very much in the way when I am climbing about from tree to tree. Today, listening to your interesting conversation, I quite forgot it, and left it behind when I came off with you. If only you had spoken in time I should have remembered it, and should have brought it along with me.'

The jellyfish was very disappointed when he heard this because he believed everything that the monkey said. The monkey was of no use if he didn't have a liver. Finally, the jellyfish stopped and told the monkey as such.

'Well,' the monkey said, 'that is soon remedied. I am really sorry to think of all your trouble, but if you will only take me back to the place where you found me, I shall soon be able to get my liver.'

The jellyfish did not like that idea at all, having to go all the way back to the island again, but the monkey assured him that if he would be so kind as to take him back he would get his very best liver, and bring it with him the next time. The jellyfish was persuaded and turned his course towards the Monkey Island once more.

No sooner had the jellyfish gotten to the shore than that sly little monkey landed, and getting up into his pine tree where he had first been found, he cut several capers amongst the branches with joy at being safe and sound at home once more, and then looked down at the jelly-fish and said,

'So many thanks for all the trouble you have taken. Please present my compliments to the Dragon King on your return.'

The jellyfish started to wonder about this speech and the mocking tone in which it was said. Then he asked the monkey if it had been his intention to come with him at once after he got his liver. The monkey laughed in response, saying that he could not afford to lose his live as it was too precious.

'But remember your promise,' pleaded the jellyfish, now very discouraged.

'That promise was false, and anyhow it is now broken,' replied the monkey. Then he started to jeer at the jellyfish and told him that he had been deceiving him the entire time. The he did not wish to lose his life, which he certainly would have done had he gone to the Sea King's Palace to the old doctor waiting for him. Instead, he persuaded the jelly fish to return him back to his island under false pretenses.

'Of course, I won't give you my liver, but come and get it if you can,' the monkey added mockingly from the tree.

There was nothing for the jellyfish to do now but to repent of his stupidity, and to return to the Dragon King of the Sea and to confess his failure. So he started to make his slow, sad swim back. The last thing he heard as he swam away, leaving Monkey Island behind him was the monkey laughing at him.

Meanwhile, the Dragon King, the doctor, the chief steward, and all of the servants were impatiently waiting for the return of the jellyfish. When they caught sight of him approaching the Palace, the hailed him with delight. They started to thank he profusely for all of the trouble he had been through to go to Monkey Island, and then they asked him where the monkey was located.

The day of reckoning had finally come for the jellyfish. He shook all over as he recounted what had happened to him. How he had gotten the monkey about halfway to the Palace, and then stupidly let the secret out about what he was doing. Then he told them how the monkey had deceived him by making him think that he had left his liver behind.

The Dragon King's wrath was great, and he at once gave orders for the jellyfish to be severely punished for incompetence. The punishment was a horrible one. All of the bones were to be taken out of his living body, and he was to be beaten with sticks.

The poor jellyfish was horrified and humiliated beyond all words, and cried out for pardon. But the Dragon King's order had to be obeyed. The servants of the Palace each brought out at stick and surrounded the jellyfish, and after they pulled out off of his bones, they beat him to a flat pulp, and then took him out past the gates of the Palace and threw him into the water. Here was left to repent and suffer his foolish chattering, and to grow accustomed to his new state of bonelessness.

Since this day, the jellyfish has had to live without the bones that his ancestors once had. They can easily be seen today thrown around by the high waves upon the shores of Japan."

CHAPTER 18

The Story of Princess Hase

"A long time ago in the city of Nara which was at one time the ancient Capital of Japan lived a wise minister whose name was Prince Toyonari Fjuiwara. He had a wife who was a beautiful, good, and noble woman whose name was Princess Murasaki which translates into Violet. Their families arranged their marriage according to the custom during that time. They had lived happy together since then. They were very sorrowful because they had not had any children in their marriage. They wanted a child that would bring joy to them in their old age, carry on the family name, and keep their ancestral rites once they died.

The Prince and his wife talked a long time and finally decided to make a trip to the temple of Hase no Kwannon or the Goddess of Mercy at Hase. According to their religion's traditions that Kwannon, the Mother of Mercy, would answer the prayers of mortals for what they needed the most. Surely after all the years they prayed and prayed, she would come to them and give them a child in answer to their prayers for their long pilgrimage since it was their biggest need. They had everything else they needed in life but it was nothing since their hearts cried for a child.

The Prince and his wife traveled to the temple of Kwannon at Hase and they remained there for a very long time. They prayed to Kwannon and offered her incense so she might feel inclined to fulfill their prayers. To their surprise, their prayers were finally answered.

At last the day came when Princess Murasaki gave birth to their daughter and joy filled her heart. When she presented the child to her husband, they decided to name her Hase Hima or the Princess of Hase since she was a gift from the Kwannon. They both raised her with great tenderness and care and the child grew in beauty and strength.

Once the girl was five, her mother grew very ill and all of the medicine and doctors in the kingdom couldn't save her. Right before she drew her last breath, she called her daughter to her. While Princess Murasaki stroked Princess Hase's hair she said, 'Hase Hima, do you know that your mother cannot live any longer? Though I die, you must grow up to be a good girl. Do your best not to give trouble to your nurse or any other of your family. Perhaps your father will marry again and someone will take my place as your mother. If so, do not grieve for me, but look at your father's second wife as your real mother, and be obedient and dutiful to both her and your father. Remember when you are grown up to be submissive to the people who are your superiors, and to be kind to all those who are under you. Don't forget this. I die with hope that you will grow up a model woman.'

Hase Hima listened with respect while her mother was talking to her and promised to do all that she wished even though she was still too young to completely understand what a great loss it was to lose her mother. There is an old proverb that states: 'As the soul is at three so it is at one hundred.' Hase Hime grew up as her mother wished. She was an obedient and good Princess.

It wasn't long after her mother died that her father Prince Toyonari did marry again. The lady was of noble birth and her name was Princess Terute. She was completely different than Princess Murasaki as this woman had a bad heart and was very cruel. She didn't love her step-daughter at all and was very unkind to Princess Hase. She was usually heard saying:

'This is not my child! This is not my child!'

But Hase Hima bore all the unkindness from her step-mother with patience. She waited upon her step-mother and obeyed everything she said. Princess Hase never gave Lady Terute any trouble just like her mother had trained her so Lady Terute didn't have any cause to complain about her.

The small Princess was very diligent and she loved studying poetry and music. She would spend countless hours every day practicing. Her father had the best teachers he could find to teach her how to play the Japanese harp or koto and the art of writing verse and letters. By the time she was 12 years old, she could play so wonderfully that Princess Hase and Lady Terute were asked to come to the Palace to perform for the Emperor.

It was during the Festival of the Cherry Flowers that he had asked them to come. the Emperor always threw himself into the festivities and asked Princess Hase to perform for him on the koto and asked Lady Terute to accompany her on the flute.

The Emporer sat himself on his raised dais behind a curtain of finely sliced bamboo and purple tassels so the he could see everything without being seen. Ordinary people were not allowed to look at his sacred face.

Hase Hime was a very skilled musician even though she was still very young. She would often astonish her teachers by her great talent and memory. During this momentous occasion she played very well but Lady Terute, was very lazy and didn't practice the flute like Hase did and she broke down during the song and requested one of the ladies of the Court to take her place. This was a huge disgrace and she was extremely jealous when she thought of the way she failed when her small step-daughter has succeeded so greatly. To make matters even worse, the Emperor sent many wonderful gifts to Princess Hase to reward her for playing so beautifully at the festivities.

Lady Terute soon gave birth to a son and this make her hate Princess Hase even more for she thought if the Princess wasn't around then her son would get all of Prince Toyonari's love.

Since she had never been taught to control herself, this wicked thought kept growing in her mind until it turned into an intense desire to kill Princess Hase.

She secretly ordered some poison to be brought to their home and she poisoned some sweet wine. She poured the poisoned wine into a bottle. She poured good wine into another bottle that looked similar. It happened that the 5th of May was coming upon them and the Boys' Festival would soon be celebrated. When the festival rolled around Hase was playing with her brother. All of his heroes and warrior toys were spread out before him and she was telling him terrific stories about all of them. They were both having lots of fun and laughing merrily with their nurses when Lady Terute entered with the bottles of wine and some cakes.

'You are both so happy and good,' said the wicked Lady Terute while smiling. 'I have brought you some sweet wine to reward you. Here are some cakes for my sweet children.'

She filled two cups one from each bottle.

Hase never thought that her step-mother would act so wicked that she took one of the cups of wine and handed it to her little brother.

Lady Terute had marked the bottles carefull but when she came into the room she got nervous and poured the wine in a hurry and had unconsciously given her child the poisoned wine. During this time, she had been watching the Princess nervously and she was amazed when she didn't see any change to the Princess. All of a sudden her child screamed in pain and threw himself onto the floor. He was doubled up in lots of pain. Lady Terute ran to him making sure she spilled the two bottles of wine as she went. She picked him up out of the floor. The nurses ran for the doctor but nothing could save her child. He died in one hour while his mother was holding him. Doctors didn't know all that much during those ancient times and they just thought the wine had disagreed with the boy and cuased him to have convulsions and that's what killed him.

Lady Terute was punished because she lost her own child while trying to kill her step-daughter. Rather than blaming herself she starting blaming Princess Hase. She began hating the princess more and more and watched for any opportunity to harm her but for this she would have to wait a long time.

When Princess Hase turned 13, she had already become a poetess of merit. This was quite an accomplishment. This was an accomplishment that was held in very high esteem by the women of ancient Japan.

During the rainy season, floods were reported daily and were doing a lot of damage to the neighborhood. The Tatsuta River that flowed through the Imperial Palace was swollen to the top of its banks. All the rolling torrents of water that was rushing along the narrow bed disturbed the Emperor so much that he was worried both night and day. It even caused a massive nervous disorder. They sent out an Imperial Edict to all the Buddhist temples asking the priests to send up constant prayers to the Heavens to stop the flood. This was done to no avail.

Within the circles of the Court, whispers began going around that Princess Hase, Prince Toyonari's daughter was a very gifted poetess even though she was still quite young. Her teachers confirmed this report.

Many years before Princess Hase, a gifted and beautiful poetess moved Heaven by praying in verse. She had brought rain down on a famished land, as was stated by the ancient biographers about the poetess Ono no Komachi.

They thought that if Princess Hase would write a poem and then offer it as a prayer, it might stop the noise coming from the rushing waters and get rid of the Imperial illness. All that the Court had said finally reached the Emperor's ears and he sent an order to Prince Toyonari.

Princess Hase's astonishment and fear was great when her father sent for her and told her what the Emperor wanted her to do. She had a very important duty to do as she was supposed to save the Emperor's life.

She finally finished her poem. She had written it on a piece of paper that had been flecked with gold. She went to the banks of the roaring river with some Court officials and her father. She raised her heart to the Heavens and she read the poem that she had written. She read it loud and pushed it heavenwards with her hands.

It seemed very strange to all the people who were standing around but the waters soon ceased their roaring and the river became quiet in answer to her prayer. The Emperor soon recovered from his nervous condition.

The Emperor was so pleased that he sent for Princess Hase to come to his Palace. He rewarded her with the title of Chinjo or Lieutenant General to show her distinction. From this point on people called her Chinjo-hime or the Lieutenant General Princess. She was loved and respected by everyone.

There was just one person who wasn't pleased with her success. And that person was her step-mother. She was still brooding over the death of her beloved son that she had killed when trying to poison the Princess. She was mortified to see the Princess rise to honor and power and be marked by Imperial favor. She was admired by the entire court. The jealousy and envy burned hot in her heart like a fire. She told many lies about the Princess to her husband but to no use. He wouldn't listen to any of her lies. He told her very sharply that she was very mistaken.

Lady Terute finally seized an opportunity while her husband was away and ordered on old servant to take the Princess into the Hibari Mountains and to kill her. This is one of the wildest parts of the country. She made up a story about the Princess that she told to her servant saying this was the only way she could keep the Princess from disgracing the family.

Katoda, Lady Terute's vassal had always been a loyal servant to his mistress and he knew it would be wisest to pretend he was obeying her command. He put Princess Hase in a palanquin and went with her to the most remote place that he could find. Princess Hase knew it wouldn't do her any good to protest to her step-mother about the way she was being treated, so she went like she was told.

The servant knew the young Princess was innocent of all the things her step-mother had accused her of and he was determined to save the Princess's life. If he didn't kill her, he couldn't return to his mistress, so he decided to stay in the wilderness and take care of the Princess. With the help of some peasants, he built himself a small cottage. He secretly sent for his wife to come be with him and the Princess. She knew in her heart that her father would come find her as soon as he returned from his trip.

Prince Toyonari, after several weeks, returned home. Lady Terute told him that Princess Hase had done something horrible and had run away because she was afraid of being punished. He was ill with anxiety. Everybody in the house told him the same story and nobody knew why the Princess left or where she had gone. Since he was worried about a scandal, he kept all this quiet and looked everywhere he could think of but still couldn't find her.

One day while he was trying to forget his worries, he called all his men to him and told them to get ready for a hunt in the mountains. They were soon packed and ready to go. They were mounted and waiting at the gate for him. He rode hard and fast to the Hibari Mountains with his men following him. He was soon far ahead of all his men and he found himself in a very beautiful valley.

He looked all around him and admired the beautiful scenery. He saw a small house on one of the hills closest to him and he heard a beautiful voice reading out loud. Curiosity took over and he wondered how could be studying so diligently out in the wilderness so far. He dismounted and left his horse with his groom. He walked up the hill and slowly got closer to the cottage. As he got closer to the cottage his surprise increase because he could finally see the person reading was a beautiful girl. The cottage door was open and she was sitting where she could see the view. He listened attentively while she was reading Buddhist scriptures with honest devotion. His curiosity kept increasing and he hurried to the gate and entered the garden. He looked up and saw his daughter the Princess Hase. She was so intent on what she way saying the she didn't see or hear her father until he spoke.

'Hase Hime!' he cried. 'It is you, my Hase Hime!'

Taken completely by surprise, she almost didn't realize that it was her father who was calling to her and for a moment she was totally incapable of being able to move or speak.

'My father! My father! It is indeed you – oh, my father!' was the only thing Princess Hase was able to say. She ran to him and grab his sleeve. She buried her face and burst into tears.

Her father held her and stroked her hair. He asked her to tell him what had happened but she was only able to cry and he began wondering if he was just dreaming.

Then Katoda came outside and bowed himself to the ground before the Prince. He poured out the tale of what Lady Terute had done and told him how his daughter came to be living in the wilderness.

The Prince could no longer hold back his indignation and astonishment. He forgot about hunting and went home at once with Princess Hase. One of his men galloped ahead of them to inform the household of the happy news. Lady Terute heard what had happened and was scared to meet her husband. She knew that her wickedness had been discovered. She fled the house and went back to her father in disgrace. Nothing was ever heard of her again.

Katoda and his wife were highly rewarded and he was given a promotion to be a part of the Prince's personal servants. He lived happily with the Prince for the rest of his days and was always devoted to the Princess. She never forgot that she would always owe her life to him and his wife. She was never bothered by an unkind step-mother ever again and she lived quietly and happily with her father.

Since Prince Toyonari didn't have a son, he found a young boy of one of the Court nobles to marry his daughter and become his heir. In a few years, they were married. Princess Hase lived for many, many years and everyone that knew her said that she was the most devout, wisest, and beautiful Princess that had ever reigned in Prince Toyonari's ancient home. She was filled with joy to be able to present her son to her father right before he decided to retire from active duty. Her son would be the future Lord of their family.

There is a preserved piece of needlework in one of the Buddhist temples in Kyoto. It is the most beautiful piece of tapestry, on it is a figure of Buddha that was embroidered in silky threads that were obtained from a lotus flower. This is said to have been embroidered by the Princess Hase herself. This would be a wonderful piece of tapestry to see if it really does exist."

CONCLUSION

Thank you for making it through to the end of the book. I hope that you have found the book informative as well as entertaining. These myths are timeless and can be enjoyed time and time again. They can also be a source of inspiration if you are planning a trip to Japan. See if you can find some of the real life inspirations for these stories.

Finally, if you found this book useful in any way, a review on Amazon is always appreciated!